# OOHRAH!

## by Bekah Brunstetter

A SAMUEL FRENCH ACTING EDITION

SAMUEL FRENCH
FOUNDED 1830

SAMUELFRENCH.COM

ISBN 978-0-573-69795-1          Printed in U.S.A.          #29263

## MUSIC USE NOTE

## IMPORTANT BILLING AND CREDIT REQUIREMENTS

*OOHRAH!* was produced by the Atlantic Theater Company (Neil Pepe, artistic director; Jeffory Lawson, managing director) at the Atlantic Stage 2 during September 2009. The performance was directed by Evan Cabnet, with sets by Lee Savage, costumes by Jessica Wegener, lighting by Tyler Micoleau, and sound by Broken Chord Collective. The production stage manager was Jillian M. Oliver, the fight director was J. David Brimmer, production manager, Michael Wade; general manager, Jamie Tyrol; associate artistic director, Christian Parker. The cast was as follows:

**ABBY** . . . . . . . . . . . . . . . . . . . . . . . . . . . . . . . . . . . . . . . . . . . . . . . Cassie Beck
**LACEY** . . . . . . . . . . . . . . . . . . . . . . . . . . . . . . . . . . . . . . . . . . . . . Sami Gayle
**RON** . . . . . . . . . . . . . . . . . . . . . . . . . . . . . . . . . . . . . . . . . . . Darren Goldstein
**POP POP** . . . . . . . . . . . . . . . . . . . . . . . . . . . . . . . . . . . . . . . . . . . . . J R Horne
**SARA** . . . . . . . . . . . . . . . . . . . . . . . . . . . . . . . . . . . . . . . . . . . . . Jennifer Mudge
**CHRISTOPHER**. . . . . . . . . . . . . . . . . . . . . . . . . . . . Lucas Near-Verbrugghe
**CHIP** . . . . . . . . . . . . . . . . . . . . . . . . . . . . . . . . . . . . . . . . . . Maximillian Osinki

# CHARACTERS

**ABBY** - Late-20s. A stewardess.

**RON** - Mid-30s. A captain in the US Army. At home: a lover and father and squash planter.

**SARA** - Mid-30s. Petite, pretty. Abby's sister. Trophy wife of Ron. Simple.

**LACEY** - Ron and Sara's 14 year-old daughter, a future US Marine.

**CHRISTOPHER** - Mid-20s. Skinny. The modern young man: pale, technologically advanced. A security guard at the local airport. Scared of most things.

**CHIP** - Early 20s. Large forced muscles. A high and tight. A lifer.

**POP POP** - Sara and Abby's aged grandfather, a veteran. He suffers from dementia, as old veterans do. Or does he just choose to seem more far away than he actually is?

# TIME/PLACE

Now; Fayetteville, North Carolina: a military town, and an airplane above it. The Southern accent is slight like an afterthought.

# ACT I

## I.

*(Sisters **SARA** and **ABBY** are in a bright modest kitchen. **SARA** is stuffing cookies into UPS boxes. The cookies are obviously homemade. In a bad way.)*

*(On the table, a spread of boxes of band aids, deodorant, bubble gum.)*

*(**ABBY** holds a package of baby butt wipes. She opens it and inspects one. She sniffs it. When she does so, we catch the light of her newly worn engagement ring, which she is not used to wearing.)*

**SARA.** *(happy)* By the time these get over there, they won't really be cookies any more but they'll like them just the same, they'll eat them like hot potata chips!

**ABBY.** Yeah.

**SARA.** They need em though, helps them get through it and keep morale up. Little piece of home. Lacey's so sweet, she's like DADDY's FRIENDS GONNA EAT THESE, DADDY GONNA EAT THESE IN THE SAND WITH THEIR GUNS! And I'm like yes, Lacey, yeah they are!

*(worried)*

Oh, I hope they like nuts!

*(**ABBY** laughs.)*

**ABBY.** Haha – nuts.

**SARA.** You're stupid.

*(**ABBY** rubs a baby wipe tentatively on her arm.)*

Hay, leave those alone, come on, those are for the boxes!

*(They stuff.)*

7

**ABBY.** Like 80 percent of men don't like mayonnaise or mayonnaise based substances cause it reminds them of, you know what. Except gay guys, I read, gay guys freakin *love* it, put it on everything. Like on toast. By itself. And on crackers.

(**ABBY** *studies the wipe.*)

What are these for?

**SARA.** Sometimes they don't get to shower for like, days, so they're *helpful.* It's awful, really, a person not getting to *bathe,* can you believe it?

**ABBY.** They're gonna rub these on their nuts?

**SARA.** *(grabbing the box)* They're goin to CLEAN themselves with them, okay? God.

*(pause)*

**ABBY.** Chris loves mayonnaise.

**SARA.** These cookies look like sad *shit.* I followed the recipe and everything! Why does everything I make turn to shit?

**ABBY.** How many boxes we doing?

**SARA.** I told Miss Israel we'd do sixty for the church. Then ten more for Danny and his friends.

**ABBY.** Danny sucks.

**SARA.** He does NOT.

**ABBY.** He hasn't sent me an email in like MONTHS.

**SARA.** He's in a war, okay, he's not sittin around like *oooh, I got a lot to say to my sister! I better say it!*

**ABBY.** Okay, fine, ten for Dan and his friends.

**SARA.** Then we gotta make 4 more batches for Lacey's party.

**ABBY.** Isn't that not til next Sunday?

**SARA.** Rachel Raye says to get started *early,* okay, she says to freeze them and then you'll have less to be stressed out about when the party comes!

**ABBY.** Okay, okay –

**SARA.** I can't *believe* Ron's gonna miss her comin out party, It's really too bad, Lacey's real sad about that.

**ABBY.** Well you could wait til next year when he's back for good.

**SARA.** I don't wanna wait, I wanna do do it *NOW.*

*(a moment)*

**ABBY.** We're gonna be here all day.

**SARA.** You got someplace else to be?

**ABBY.** No, it's okay.

**SARA.** Got plans with Chris?

**ABBY.** *(not stuffing)* No.

**SARA.** If you're gonna stay here, you gotta help.

**ABBY.** What the *hell!*

**SARA.** What?

**ABBY.** IF I'm gonna stay here? I'm stayin here to HELP while / Ron is gone!

**SARA.** I *know.*

**ABBY.** You said you didn't wanna be alone, you're the one who asked ME to stay here, I'm just saying.

**SARA.** I'm glad you're here, okay? Damn.

*(Pause. They stuff.* **ABBY** *is clearly somewhere else.)*

**SARA.** No I mean it, I really am. Don't know what I'd do if you weren't here.

**ABBY.** Yeah, right.

**SARA.** I'd talk to myself, that's what I'd do. Or I'd leave the TV on all day for noise and I'd talk back to it. God I hate being alone.

**ABBY.** I think being alone is nice sometimes.

**SARA.** We should bring Pop Pop over for dinner.

**ABBY.** Yeah.

**SARA.** He doesn't like that new home. They don't treat him nice, they treat him like a baby. And I'm like, we're payin you an arm and a leg, you better treat him like a *king.*

ABBY. Mom and DAD're payin an arm and a leg.

SARA. But still. He doesn't like it there, that's all I'm sayin.

ABBY. He doesn't know *what* he likes.

SARA. Well, I'm gonna sign him out and bring him over for dinner, I don't like to think about him there by himself. And we promised Mom we would, it's been too long.

ABBY. They're only in Greensboro, they could look in on him too.

SARA. That's over an hour drive, Ab, they've got stuff to do.

ABBY. Pop Pop makes me sad, old people make me sad.

SARA. I know.

> (**ABBY** *shrugs. Pause. A cookie crumbles.*)

These cookies're goin so far. All the way across the ocean.

The other day I was like, how far have I been?

You've been real far, you been everywhere. Las Vegas, Santa Fe. New York.

ABBY. I don't really get off the plane, it doesn't count. I just kinda look at it through the window like *hey, look at that.*

SARA. Yeah, but you've been there, your body has been in the place, over it, yeah, *(Pause. They stuff.)* Virginia! That's how far I've been. And that doesn't even count cause that's just where I was born.

ABBY. Mom took us to Florida when you were like four.

SARA. How do you know?

ABBY. Pictures.

SARA. Alright, I been to Florida.

ABBY. Tommorrow I'm doing a flight all the way to California, first time.

SARA. Damn, how long does that take?

ABBY. Five hours.

SARA. Damn.

(**ABBY** *absently stuffs. She stops, shoves a cookie in her mouth.* **SARA** *absently swats her hand.* **ABBY** *picks the cookie back up, continues eating it.*)

**SARA.** So how's Chris taking all the wedding plans, is he freaking out yet?

**ABBY.** He's beein all girly about it. *Abby, what about a carrot cake with little cupcakes around it for everybody! Ab, what about a live accordion player? Ab, what about for the rehearsal dinner everybody just plays laser tag!!*
I'm like Chris, we haven't even picked a date yet, and he's all PICK A DATE, I LOVE YOU and I'm like I'M GOING TO IF YOU'D JUST LET ME BREATHE FOR A MINUTE!

(*beat*)

**SARA.** Are you excited?

**ABBY.** Yeah –

**SARA.** Yeah?

**ABBY.** (*feigning, trying*) I mean, yeah, it's gonna be great. We're gonna have house that's just ours. I never had like, a house. With grown up stuff in it. All new appliances. A pull out couch for guests, a deck with a grill. New bedroom furniture, a walk in closet. Chris wants to get a dog and I think I might get a sewing machine. I wanna make pillows, I think. Kiss that face, forever.

**SARA.** He loves you.

**ABBY.** So?

**SARA.** What'd you mean, *So?*

**ABBY.** (*hot*) So nobody else's gonna love me ever?

**SARA.** ...I didn't say that, I'm just sayin, I think he's nice.

**ABBY.** Jesus is nice, should I give Jesus a blowjob?

(*pause*)

**SARA.** You okay?

**ABBY.** Last night we were doin it, I started to cry.

**SARA.** Aw, cause you were happy?

**ABBY.** No.

Cause sometimes I think I'd rather die than do it with him but I do it anyways. I pretended I was happy then went to the bathroom and cried some more then said it was my contacts and we went to sleep.

**SARA.** Why do you do it, then, if you hate it so much?

**ABBY.** Cause he loves me.

**SARA.** You're thinking bout it too much.

**ABBY.** Yeah, yeah, I know. *(pause)* I don't like it when he touches me. His kisses are too small, like I'm doin a kitten, that's not sexy. I wanna be thrown around.

(**SARA** *giggles.*)

**SARA.** Oh HUSH.

**ABBY.** *(smiling)* Yeah, picked up and thrown all around.

**SARA.** STOP it.

**ABBY.** I *do.*

*(pause)*

Like um, like what's it like – with you and Ron?

**SARA.** I'm *not* gonna talk like that.

**ABBY.** I'm just curious.

*(pause)*

**SARA.** *(warm, remembering)* It's good. It's real good.

**ABBY.** Like what?

**SARA.** Like when you're like 14 and you're day dreamin about somebody, some senior with green eyes and big arms, like the first time you dream that he – pushes you up against your locker –

**ABBY.** Somebody big and strong –

**SARA.** Yeah and he picks you up / and

**ABBY.** Yeah and just *puts* you somewhere.

*(They imagine this together.)*

**ABBY.** You always got all the good ones. The good ones never wanted me.

*(Uncomfortable, **SARA** shakes this off, begins to clean up.)*

**ABBY.** Hay, isn't Lacey kinda young to debut or whatever?

**SARA.** Whadda *you* know about it? You didn't even come out.

**ABBY.** Neither did *you*.

**SARA.** Well Lacey got her first period, okay, So I figure she's old enough! It was the sweetest thing, she's all embarrassed about it, she left an empty box a tampons on my bed, with a little note *Mom I need more a these.* She won't talk about it.

**ABBY.** That's weird.

**SARA.** What?

**ABBY.** Have people over cause she got her period. Like YAY, PERIOD PARTY!

**SARA.** It's her *birthday.*

Plus I want every one to see the house. Plus I always wanted a party, you know? I just want something nice to look forward to.

**ABBY.** Mom wasn't in to all that, it was hard enough to get her to put pants on when someone came over.

**SARA.** Screw *that,* I think Lacey should get a nice pretty party.

**ABBY.** Is that what she wants?

**SARA.** She'll get it and she'll like it, that's what. OOH! HAY! Look what I got for the party! *(She grabs a big shopping bag.)* Did I show you what I got at Party City?! Look look look!

*(She digs into the bag and pulls out pink streamers, decorations, candles.)*

33 and a half percent off, all of it!

*(She lines everything up neatly on the table, inspects it, proudly.)*

AND AND AND –

*(From the bag, she retrieves a pink, sparkly tiara. She holds it out for* **ABBY**'s *inspection. A price tag dangles from it. She rips it off.* **ABBY** *takes it.)*

**SARA.** *(cont.)* Isn't it the most darling thing?

(**ABBY** *inspects it, looks a little disgusted.*)

**ABBY.** You think *Lacey's* gonna wear this?

**SARA.** *(looking at crown) I* think it's precious. And important and nice.
And I wish Ron could be here, that's all, I just wish he was here for it.

(*She puts it back in the bag. She reaches for a cigarette, offers one to* **ABBY.** **ABBY** *shakes her head.*)

**SARA.** You're no fun since you quit, you make me feel bad.

**ABBY.** Your teeth're yellow like little fucking pieces of Dell Monte canned corn.

**SARA.** They are NOT.

**ABBY.** Well, they should be. It's not fair that they're not, cause mine are.

(**SARA** *shrugs. She lights a cigarette, blowing it out the window.*)

**SARA.** It's just cause I don't really smoke, just when I'm STRESSED. Just leftovers from high school, I gotta do SOMETHIN I'm not supposed to.

(*She picks tobacco from her tongue, breathing deep.*)

**SARA.** I'm gonna quit too.

(*She exhales.*)

Whenever he's gone, I smoke so many cigarettes I can feel my heart move.

(*She contemplates this.*)

Holy shit, I miss him.

(*She sucks this angst through her cigarette, exhaling hard.*)

**ABBY.** You miss him when he's gone, like really?

**SARA.** So bad. Even when it's just a day or a weekend.

**ABBY.** When Chris went to that comic book convention thing I dreamt his plane went down.

**SARA.** Good thing it didn't.

**ABBY.** Yeah, good thing. *(beat)*

And the waiting is – when you wait for him – I bet the waiting's good, right? Sitting by the window, waiting, all full of – lust – I guess –

**SARA.** It was worse when he was deployed the first time cause I was pregnant and miserable and all alone but that was more like, *why the hell are you not here* more so than anything romantic at all. But yeah, it is kinda good.

Mainly I just want him to get back and stay back so I can start my damn life finally, start our life together, no more waiting. It's gonna be so great.

**ABBY.** What is?

**SARA.** *(like she's read it somewhere)* Stability.

*(beat)*

**ABBY.** And you get real – excited about him? About Ron? I mean, down there, in your, you –

**SARA.** STOP it.

**ABBY.** No, I didn't mean – I just mean – how do you guys usually – I mean do you usually – how many times? Like in a weekend, how many times?

**SARA.** That's weird. You're weird.

**ABBY.** I was kidding.

**SARA.** No, you weren't.

*(A door opens and shuts, hard. The sound of boots.)*

**RON.** *(O.S.)* ANYBODY HOME?

*(SARA drops her cigarette, eyes wide.)*

**SARA.** Oh my God, It's RON!!!!

*(She makes a mad dash for the door.)*

*(ABBY sits.)*

**ABBY.** *(softly)* I want a soldier. I want one too, yeah.

## II.

*(The bedroom of a 14 year-old girl. Inside of it, a 14 year-old girl.)*

*(**LACEY** has sprouted awkward boobs. She wears her Dad's old desert fatigues, pants very cuffed, and stands in front of a mirror, presumably. She holds a broom handle as a rifle.)*

*(Softy, to herself, she is singing the fighting hymn of the US Marines.)*

**LACEY.** *(singing badly, marching slightly)*

From the Halls of Montezuma

To the shores of Tripoli

We fight our country's battles

In the air, on land, and sea;

First to fight for right and freedom

And to keep our honor clean;

We are proud to claim the title

Of United States Marine.

*(She stops marching. She stands at attention sticking out her chest. She sees her chest, then sinks it back in. She wields her gun.)*

Pow.

*(Her cell phone rings. She answers.)*

Sup Chelsea.

Nothing, just painting my nails. Green. No, I took it off.

What's at the mall? I'm *sick* of the mall. *(She spits.)*

My mom can't drive, she's doing something for church, Your mom'll have to drive, maybe my mom could pick up.

Whaddayou mean am I still your friend, of course I'm your friend! You're the one that's not MY friend. You haven't called me in like FOUR days.

LACEY. *(cont.)* Wh – I'm not being a bitch, YOU'RE being a bitch. Yeah, no YOU are.

You think I care what people SAY? What, um, what do they say?

F *that*, nobody said that.

Ever – ever since – lemee *talk*. LEMMEE TALK! *(She yells into phone.)* JUST BECAUSE WE'RE IN HIGH SCHOOL NOW DOESN'T MEAN TO HAVE TO BE SUCH A BITCH.

It's gone to your head. Yes it HAS. You're shallow. You're like the shallow end. I'm not gonna stoop to you level, I got moral fibers.

I AM NOT DIFFERENT ALL THE SUDDEN, *YOU'RE* DIFFERENT ALL THE SUDDEN!

*EVERYTHING's* DIFFERENT ALL OF THE SUDDEN!

You're a sow! A sow is a lady PIG!

*(She hangs up and throws her phone. She is near tears. RON appears in the doorway, watching her. He is late 30's, buff as hell. She grabs her broom again. She aims. She shoots.)*

Bam.

RON. *(softly)* What you doin?

*(LACEY turns around and sees her dad. She drops the broom.)*

LACEY. DADDY! What're you doin here??

*(She rushes to him, throws her arms around him ferociously. Then, self conscious, and sensing his discomfort, she pulls away.)*

Hay, Daddy.

RON. Hay.

LACEY. You're back early!

RON. I know.

What're you doin, what's all this?

LACEY. I – I'm wearin your coat.

RON. S'alright.

LACEY. I didn't know you were gonna be back so soon – I was gonna have stuff ready to show you, but I don't have anything ready –

RON. Look at you. You're big!

LACEY. I grew.

RON. I guess you did, yeah! Let me look at you, hold still.

LACEY. Okay –

(*LACEY shifts uncomfortably as* RON *looks at her, inspects her.*)

RON. Got your ears, got your nose, full head a hair, yep – okay, all's in order – Let'see here –

(*He starts to tickle her, like he used to.*)

LACEY. (*laughing*) Stop it Daddy, stop!

(*The tickling escalates.*)

STOP IT, DAD!

(**RON** *stops, unaccustomed to her outburst. He clears his throat.* **LACEY** *regains herself.*)

LACEY. I – I wanna be a Marine, I think.

RON. What's wrong with the army?

LACEY. Marines are first to fight.

RON. Baby I know what a Marine is.

LACEY. I just think they're cool, that's all.

RON. Last I saw you, you were beggin' your Mom for second holes in your ears and crying over trips to Carowinds.

LACEY. I saw a commercial and went to the website.

RON. Okay, alright –

LACEY. And I had this dream where I was fightin with you and I wasn't scared.

RON. You did?

LACEY. Yeah. Did you have any dreams about me?

RON. Course.

LACEY. Maybe we were dreaming about each other at the same time.

**RON.** Could be.

*(***LACEY*** *looks at him. She is a little girl again, throws her arms around him, hugging him tight. He doesn't know what to do, so he gingerly puts his arms around her.)*

**LACEY.** *(into his chest)* I got so much to tell you –

**RON.** We got plenty a time –

**LACEY.** Don't go again, okay?

*(He kisses the top of her head. She squeezes him.)*

**RON.** S'allright now. Alright.

## III.

*(A dim, modest bedroom with intentionally placed accent pillows.)*

*(**RON** is taking off his shirt. Dogtags dangle on his chest. He looks in the mirror, rubbing the top of his head. He seems to feel out of place in the room.)*

*(**SARA**, tip toes into the room. She removes her bathrobe and is petite and simple in her wifey and slutty night-gown. She turns down the bed.)*

**SARA.** Dishwasher's broken.

**RON.** I'll take a look.

*(beat)*

**SARA.** You like what I done with the house?

**RON.** Yeah, it looks nice.

**SARA.** I wanted it to look nice for you, you've barely gotten to live in it at all. Buy me a whole house and you haven't even got to live in it yet, it's a shame!

**RON.** I wanna take that guest room and make it into a study, like with books. And a computer, and maps on the wall of all over the world, places I've been.

**SARA.** Well that's where Abby's stayin.

**RON.** Well she gonna stay here much longer?

**SARA.** She was only here to help while you were away –

**RON.** Help with what?

**SARA.** Moral support!

**RON.** Well I'm back now, and I'll morally support you, okay? It's crowded, it was crowded at the dinner table.

**SARA.** You want her to go?

**RON.** She's your sister, it's up to you. I'm just sayin, it's crowded. I just want space, that's all. I wanna get all settled, I'm ready, I got big plans.

**SARA.** How do you say that to your own sister, to get the hell out?

**RON.** I don't know, baby, I don't have any sisters. Good thing, too. I'd a killed them.

**SARA.** I wish you did, you'd probably be sweeter sometimes. More sensitive.

*(beat)*

Lacey's got boobs now, you see that?

*(RON nods.)*

I think her whole Marine kick's a phase, I mean, it's cute and all, kids go through phases, I mean, when I was her age I wanted to be an ice skater one minute and a ballerina the next.

**RON.** I think it's kinda cool.

**SARA.** Oh you do, huh?

**RON.** I do.

**SARA.** She wrote an essay about you for school!

**RON.** Oh yeah?

**SARA.** I put it on the fridge.

Its just that she's all different now all a the sudden. It makes me kinda sad like I don't know her anymore. I come home last week, she's cut all her hair off with my kitchen scissors!

**RON.** She's just growin up.

**SARA.** No, she's *different*. I say Lacey, come help me make the insides of the pot pie, she says *screw you* and goes out back, shoots Dr. Pepper cans with a BB gun.

**RON.** Where'd she get a BB gun?

**SARA.** I have no idea.

*(RON chuckles.)*

**RON.** That's my girl.

**SARA.** I'm gonna sign Pop Pop out and bring him over for supper this week.

He's not doin so good, 'specially since he had that fall, he's getting farther and farther away.

**RON.** He's old, Sara. Let him be old.

*(pause)*

**SARA.** Why you gotta be mean to me tonight?

**RON.** I'm not bein mean.

**SARA.** Be sweet.

**RON.** I *AM*.

**SARA.** No you're not. You've barely said a word to me since you got home. You never say enough things.

**RON.** I'm not – used to – I've said plenty a words.

**SARA.** Just a buncha little ones, they don't count.

*(He stops what he's doing, grabs her, husbandly, kisses her.)*

**RON.** I'm real happy to be home.

**SARA.** For good this time, for real?

**RON.** For good. I let em know, no more tours.

**SARA.** Promise?

**RON.** Uh huh.

**SARA.** So what're you gonna do?

**RON.** What?

**SARA.** What's our plan?

**RON.** I don't know exactly, but for now, gonna have picnics *(He kisses her.)* and a 401K *(He kisses her.)* and barbecues with steaks *(He kisses her.)* and a motherfuckin lake house. *(He kisses her, triumphantly.)*

**SARA.** Oh, Ron, really? Can we get a jet ski?!

**RON.** Whatever you want, baby.

**SARA.** And I want a big red minivan or maybe a little SUV!

**RON.** We'll get you whatever you want.

*(He kisses her again. She goes for it.)*

**SARA.** How was it this time, you got any boo-boo's for me to kiss?

*(He pulls away, subtly. So, she stops too, self-consciously.)*

It's okay, gotta shower first, I'm all gross down there.
I didn't even know you were comin, I wasn't prepared.
I was gonna get a new duvet.

**RON.** I thought you'd like the surprise so I surprised you. I thought it was some romance.

*(Pause. It's oddly awkward.)*

**SARA.** Well, this is just perfect timing! You're just in time for Lacey's party! You can do the grill and help with the decorations.

**RON.** Sure, okay –

**SARA.** I was gonna get it catered but then I thought hell, whatever, I'm a woman and a wife, I can do it myself. Save some money, put a homey touch to it.

**RON.** There's my girl!

**SARA.** There's still lots do. Friday I'm gonna do the grocery shoppin and cut up all the condiments and I think we need some sorta plant or ficus plant for the deck or something. And that window in the foyer? It's lonely, it needs a bench underneath it. A wooden bench that nobody'll ever sit on, with gold trim on it, I saw one at Target, it was real nice.

OOH and you finish the molding in the living room like you were going to! Then it'll be perfect. 'Member you started on them but never finished them!

**RON.** *(hard)* I haven't been here, Sara.

**SARA.** I *know.*

*(beat)*

You didn't even tell me you missed me.

**RON.** Course I missed you, who else would I miss?

**SARA.** Jeanie's husband come back and gave her herpes from an Arab prostitute, she thinks.

**RON.** Who's Jeannie?

**SARA.** She used to worked the register at Eckerds. Now she's married to Ned, from / your –

**RON.** Ned, good guy.

**SARA.** I ran into her at Food Lion, she had just come back from the gynecologist. She was standing there in the produce, holdin a cantaloupe, cryin.

**RON.** *(messing with her)* That's probably just what the doctor told her. He probably got it from a regular old prostitute.

**SARA.** STOP it, you're BAD.

*(beat)*

**SARA.** Ned didn't go anywhere this time. He stayed at home.

**RON.** I *know.*

**SARA.** I'm just sayin, okay?

**RON.** *(hard)* And what the hell difference does it make, Sara, cause I'm back now for good, alright?

*(pause)*

**SARA.** Regina from my pilates class, her husband makes real good money, he works for Krispy Kreme, he's a regional manager. *(beat)* You could do that, you could work there.

**RON.** You want me to fuckin sell doughnuts, Sara?

**SARA.** They're not JUST doughnuts RON, they're the best doughnuts ever!
Sides, You love doughnuts! It's a good job!

**RON.** *(hard, loud)* I like to eat em, I don't wanna work for em! Fuckin *shit,* Sara, just gimmee a minute!

**SARA.** HAY! Don't bring those words in here, leave that out there! I asked you not to bring that in here!
This house is a sanctuary of nice things!

**RON.** I – 'm sorry, I'm sorry –

**SARA.** I'm sorry. *(beat)* I just think you'd be real good at a job like that. Regionally managing something. Party City, they're hiring too. You took those business classes on base, right?

**RON.** That was a long time ago.

*(beat)*

**RON.** No such thing as Arab Prostitutes.

**SARA.** No?

**RON.** I didn't see any.

(**SARA** *turns off the light beside the bed.*)

(*Slowly, she walks towards him, grabbing him deliciously from behind, running her hands over his stomach, kissing his shoulder blades.*)

**SARA.** *(whispering)* Every time the phone rang I peed myself.

(*He puts his hands over hers.*)

Thinkin it was news that you're dead.

**RON.** It's alright now.

**SARA.** Lacey's asleep.

(*He reaches around and puts his hands on her ass.*)

**SARA.** If you go again I'll kill myself.

**RON.** Then who would I come back to?

(*He picks her up like a paperclip, carries her to the bed, tosses her on it. Their actions are dirty and awesome.*)

**SARA.** Last week I dreamt I made love with a baby in a car seat. I wanted you so bad, I didn't even, my brain didn't know what was what –

**RON.** Quit talking –

**SARA.** Like an actual BABY. Like MAYBE a toddler.

**RON.** I missed you so much –

**SARA.** You did?

**RON.** I don't know how to say –

(*They go for it.* **ABBY** *appears in the doorway. She watches.*)

**SARA.** Did I turn the oven off?

**RON.** Doesn't matter.

**SARA.** I didn't look at anybody else the whole time. I didn't want anybody else but you.

(*He kisses her, hard.* **ABBY** *watches with wide, hungry eyes.*)

## IV.

*(An airplane.)*

*(ABBY sits next to CHIP, who wears the crisp dress blues of a US Marine. He is sleeping against the window. Her eyes are on him. He is dreaming. The plane shakes. Quickly, he wakes up.)*

CHIP. PUT ME DOWN!

*(He shakes himself awake, eyes wide. He feels for his arms and legs.)*

ABBY. You okay?

*(He nods and straightens the sleeves of his coat, stretching out his neck.)*

ABBY. Thank you for your service.

CHIP. You're welcome.

ABBY. And for your sacrifice.

My brother's in the service so I sympathize with what you're going through.

You sure you're alright?

*(pause)*

CHIP. Yeah, I'm fine.

ABBY. Don't worry, we're almost there. We've begun our initial descent, so. We flew the whole way from California, you were asleep.

*(CHIP rubs his eyes.)*

You from California?

CHIP. Nah, I was just – stationed there. From Ohio, originally, just outside Dayton.

ABBY. We sat on the runway for an hour before we took off. You were asleep then too.

Electrical problems, they said. I don't know, I don't believe it, I think it might be bullshit on accounta gas prices and genocide and what's on the TV lately, *Sex and the City* getting cancelled, tomatoes that make you puke til you die, I personally don't believe anything anyone tells me. I've got my own code. You were fast asleep.

**ABBY.** *(cont.)* You gotta pee? It's been like 5 hours, you haven't peed once, you must have to like *bad.*

**CHIP.** I'm good, thanks.

**ABBY.** Yeah, don't go in there, it smells like wet cucumbers. They say they clean it, but I don't believe anybody.

**CHIP.** *(looking out the window)* Are we gonna fall?

**ABBY.** Probably not.

**CHIP.** ….Probably?

**ABBY.** Most likely no. You got a better chance maybe a getting struck by a car, it's safer in the air.

You ever seen *Lost*?

*(**CHIP** shakes his head no.)*

It's a TV show. Anyways, don't watch it. At least not the first part. They crash and most of them die. And when they crash, it's like they're flyin backwards. Doors ripped off the side. Masks fall from the ceiling. Crying, 200 lives passing before 400 eyes.

People say I'm real dark, but I'm not. It's mainly just when I'm on my period or something, I see things how they really are. So.

I'm on my period now, I guess I just said that.

Hell, whatever.

You're doing great. All you gotta do is relax. I like your uniform. You want a beer?

*(**CHIP** nods. She gets up. She's very obviously now a flight attendant. She fetches him a beer, brings it back, hands it to him. She sits back down next to him.)*

**CHIP.** You allowed to sit?

**ABBY.** I don't really follow rules. Do you?

**CHIP.** Yeah.

**ABBY.** I mean, I do.

*(He drinks it hungrily.)*

**ABBY.** *(cont.)* Everybody's asleep. Nothing like a shaking plane to put you right to bed, it's like a womb in here sometimes.

You comin or goin, you been over there yet?

**CHIP.** Kinda both. Haven't been, bout to go, real soon. Yeah, real soon. Headin to Fayetteville first.

**ABBY.** *(excited)* That's where I'm from!

**CHIP.** Oh yeah?

**ABBY.** That's where I live! That's where I grew up, How bout that? So what's a Marine doing in Fayetteville? On an army base?

**CHIP.** *(quickly)* Special orders.

**ABBY.** I love the Marine uniform. So regal. So much better than the army uniform. You look like something from a really good book.

**CHIP.** Soldiers, they got nothing on this uniform. Army changes their dress greens every ten years trying to keep up, they don't know what they want. Navy, they look like a buncha ice fairies in white. Marine Corps, we got the same uniform since the beginning of time.

**ABBY.** It looks really good.

*(Here, she probably crams some nuts in her mouth. She coughs. She swallows.)*

**ABBY.** My brother's over there, yeah. Been there – ten months? He's in the army, though. Danny, he's a Lieutenant. Lieutenant Danny Jim. If you see him, tell him I said hi and why doesn't he return my fuckin emails?

*(She laughs like she's never cussed before.)*

It's not like he's doin much of anything.

**CHIP.** *(defensively)* He's doin a lot.

**ABBY.** Yeah, I guess so.

*(The plane lurches. CHIP holds tight to his seat.)*

**CHIP.** Are we falling?

**ABBY.** We just hit a cloud.

**CHIP.** I'm not scared or anything.

*(He settles into his seat, drinks his beer.)*

**ABBY.** It'd be kinda silly if you were.

**CHIP.** Yeah and I'm not.

I killed a man, I'm not scared of a falling plane.

**ABBY.** *(eyes wide)* You did, really?

**CHIP.** Sort of, in boot camp.

Nah, he wasn't a real man, he was just a good imitation of one, he was made a plastic with a real life face and a beard. Nah, we're not trained to just go around killing, unless the opportunity presents itself. We're not monsters, we got integrity.

Chaplain always says, *I hope you all get your kill, you'll all get your kill.* And that's hard cause now, you never got any good reason to shoot it seems. Somebody's gotta be pointing a gun at you aiming to shoot before you can raise your own arms. You see him take out his cell phone, detinate the bomb that blows the ass off your convoy, you can't do shit but stand there and watch him do it. Since Blackwater, you can't do shit.

I killed a turtle once too but that was by accident. I scared it and it pissed itself and it drowned in it's own piss.

You ever been to California?

*(ABBY shakes her head.)*

**ABBY.** Nah, I only been above it.

I think I got family there but they don't write. I think they're Mormons or puppeteers. We don't talk to that part of the family, they might also live on a commune, I forget which.

**CHIP.** That's where they do the training lots of times, that's where I trained. They got whole little villages set up there for you to train in, break down doors. They teach you how to break down a door.

**ABBY.** Wow.

You know what's weird? It's so weird when you're on a plane, how close you are to the stranger next to you. Get off the plane, it's like you've lived your whole life together. Remember when I sat down next to you? That was eight thousand years ago.

*(The plane lurches again.* **CHIP** *screams. He then collects himself. Pause.)*

**ABBY.** You wanna hold my hand?

**CHIP.** Nah, it's okay.

**ABBY.** You can hold it if you want to.

*(***CHIP*** hesitates. The plane lurches again. He grabs* **ABBY***'s hand. He doesn't look at her. Color rushes to her face. She is in heaven.)*

## V.

*(An airport terminal.)*

*(The baggage claim. Bags go by.)*

*(**CHIP** watches diligently for his own, a sack beside him.)*

*(**CHRISTOPHER**, a security guard, meanders by on duty. He is thin and very good at video games. His uniform eats him. He has little-to-no balls. He spots **CHIP**, and is intrigued. He hovers nearby at attention, one hand on his bad-ass security guard stick.)*

**CHRISTOPHER.** Women love a man in uniform, huh?

**CHIP.** What?

**CHRISTOPHER.** Our uniforms.

**CHIP.** Oh – yeah.

**CHRISTOPHER.** Right on, man. You waiting for you luggage? *(**CHIP** nods.)* Did anyone to your knowledge tamper with it? And by tamper with it, I think I mean touch it in any way. *(**CHIP** shakes his head no.)* Yeah, I know, I'm just supposed to ask that.

You ever thrown a puppy off a cliff?

**CHIP.** What? No.

**CHRISTOPHER.** Yeah, right, I know, I know, you guys just got a bad rep.

*(pause)* I coulda been a soldier.

Nah, I couldn't have.

*(Pause. **CHIP** waits for his bag, fidgeting nervously.)*

**CHRISTOPHER.** Too many *rules*.

Rules with this job, too. I mean *rules*, right?

**CHIP.** Ha – yeah –

**CHRISTOPHER.** Around here they smoke your ass for breaking rules, for not paying attention. And by 'smoke your ass' I don't mean like murder or kill or annihilate, I mean fire. You ever been fired?

**CHIP.** Hell no.

CHRISTOPHER. Me neither.

*(pause)*

Except from my last job. It was stupid.

*(pause)*

So you're not supposed to look at porn while you're at work. So what? You remove the mild social stigma, and what's the big deal anyways? It's just two people doing it. I was lonely, you know? I'm lonely. Or I was.

Not lonely anymore though, got a fiancée. Yeah, she said yes.

CHIP. *(politely)* Congratulations.

**(CHRISTOPHER** *is bored, so he pulls out his Play-station.)*

CHRISTOPHER. You wanna play?

**(CHIP** *shakes his head No.* **CHRISTOPHER** *starts to play.)*

CHRISTOPHER. I'm TECHNICALLY not supposed to be playing games while on shift.

*(with a voice)*

GOD OF WAR.

**(CHIP** *does not respond.)*

CHAIN OF OLYMPUS.

I mean it's no *Tom Clancy's Ghost of Recon Advanced Warfighter 2*, but none too shabby my friend. One minute you're stabbing a proletariat with a fiery dagger, next thing you know you're giving a cotton wench her first orgasm. Up up downdowndowndowndowndown.

*(He plays.)*

NOICE. Grrr. Suck it.

It's kinda like *Call of Duty 4*, too, but more epic. More Greek. You sure you don't wanna play?

*(He holds it out.* **CHIP** *shakes his head No again.* **CHRISTOPHER** *continues playing.)*

CHRISTOPHER. It's not real, I know. It wasn't until I was like 12 that I realized you can't stand on a cloud.

CHIP. Why would you think that?

CHRISTOPHER. I know, I just thought so cause of Mario, I pretty much thought you could stand on them.

*(CHRISTOPHER puts game away. Eyes CHIP. He checks his insignia. Something's wrong / misplaced. CHRISTOPHER's eyes grow wide but he tries to conceal this.)*

You probably aren't into games though, am I right? You being the real deal and all, you probably prefer life. Am I right, Sargent?

They gave me this 'stick' thing.

*(He holds it up.)*

It's made of, um, I want to say something comparable to the outside of an old microwave, but in stick form. It's for in case I come across any suspicious characters, like yourself.

CHIP. Yeah and how am I suspicious?

CHRISTOPHER. You just are.

*(CHIP's bag finally comes across the belt. He grabs it, starts to go. CHRISTOPHER stands in his way.)*

CHIP. Yeah – I got – I got to *be* somewhere real soon, I got stuff to do –

CHRISTOPHER. I'm sorry to inconvenience you, sir. Or is it Lieutenant?

CHIP. PFC.

CHRISTOPHER. Private first class huh?

*(CHIP nods.)*

You got the wrong 'rank insignia' That's what it's called, right? I know some of the words.

CHIP. *(quietly)* What?

*(CHRISTOPHER clears his throat.)*

CHRISTOPHER. Your rank insignia, it's not right.

CHIP. What the fuck, man?

**CHRISTOPHER.** I'm just saying, I noticed, I happened to notice back there, I mean I have played a LOT of *Call of Duty* like mainly 2 and 3 and what you're wearing is NOT –

(**CHRISTOPHER** *moves closer to* **CHIP,** *inspecting the patches on his blues*)

Huh – interesting –

(*He reaches for one of the medals.* **CHIP** *viciously smack his hand away.*)

**CHRISTOPHER.** OW. SHIT.

(**CHRISTOPHER** *grabs his hand in pain.*)

OW, SHIT. OW.

(*He cradles it to his cheek. He goes to a corner. He kisses his hand like a kitten.*)

Ow, ow, ow, ow.

**CHIP.** *(breathing heavy)* Just back off, man.

**CHRISTOPHER.** What?

**CHIP.** *(hard)* I SAID BACK OFF.

**CHRISTOPHER.** Sir, are you causing a situation? YELLING is not, It is SO prohibited in the terminal area and baggage claim area and pretty much all areas involving the area of the airport, generally, so.

It's pretty much a matter of national security.

**CHIP.** 'Scuse me.

(*He tries to go.* **CHRISTOPHER** *steps in front of him, Bold.*)

**CHRISTOPHER.** I'm going to need to see some identification.

(**CHIP** *tries to walk past him.* **CHRISTOPHER** *stops him again.*)

(**ABBY** *passes, her hair is down, she's rolling a small suitcase behind her.*)

**ABBY.** Chris, I'm gonna head home to Sara's –

(*She spots* **CHIP.** *Then, to* **CHRISTOPHER**:)

What's goin on?

**CHRISTOPHER.** ….Nothin.

**ABBY.** Chris, what did you do?

**CHRISTOPHER.** I'm asserting my authority! I'm just doin my job!

**ABBY.** You're not / authorized to –

**CHRISTOPHER.** He's SUSPICIOUS!

**ABBY.** Chris, he's not suspicious. He's a MARINE.

**CHRISTOPHER.** So what if he is, what difference does that make?

**CHIP.** I'm kind of in a hurry – so –

**ABBY.** So, he's like a freakin PILLAR of bravery and I don't know, goodness, okay?

*(to* **CHIP***)*

I'm sorry about him, he's always playing games.

**CHRISTOPHER.** You know him?

*(This becomes couple's argument that gets slightly private.)*

**ABBY.** He was on my *flight.*

Chris, You can't go around *asserting your authority.*

**CHRISTOPHER.** Ab, I did three months of the training, okay? I am MORALLY OBLIGATED –

**ABBY.** Just – not on freaking *Marines,* okay?

**CHRISTOPHER.** *Fine.*

*(to* **CHIP***)*

I'm her fiancée. *(putting his arm around her)* Little lady said yes!

**CHIP.** *(starting to go)* S'alright.

**ABBY.** You goin to the base, you need a ride? It's right by my house, I got a car.

**CHIP.** Nah.

**ABBY.** You sure? Cab's gonna cost you 40 bucks.

*(***CHIP** *hesitates.)*

Come on.

**CHIP.** Yeah – okay.

*(He grabs his things, starts to head towards the exit.)*

**CHRISTOPHER.** I'll come over when I get off!

**ABBY.** You don't get off til midnight.

**CHRISTOPHER.** But we were gonna google honeymoons!

**ABBY.** We can do that tomorrow. I'll see you then okay?

**CHRISTOPHER.** Get some sleep, you look tired.

**ABBY.** I will.

**CHRISTOPHER.** It'll be hard not to sleep next to me but you can do it, I promise. Call me if you get scared.

*(**ABBY** can't help but smile at this. Oh, Christopher.)*

**ABBY.** Love you.

*(She kisses **CHRISTOPHER** quickly hurries after **CHIP**. **CHRISTOPHER** is left standing alone in the room with his stick.)*

**CHRISTOPHER.** I missed you!

*(pause)*

While you were gone. And stuff.

So.

See you later.

*(He sits.)*

## VI.

*(SARA and RON's kitchen, later that evening.)*

*(POP POP sits alone at the kitchen table. He holds a fork and is quiet, grinding his teeth. Someone else has dressed him. He is slightly hard to understand, as he eats his words and says them at the same time – but speaks with intense purpose.)*

**POP POP.** Hello?

Could somebody – whar'd everybody go?

*(beat)*

I was just gonna say one thing. Listen. This was – 52. I's just a *kid*.

And Mitchell – he was younger. He was scared and I's a rock.

We was all alone with the air all around us, with our wives home waitin. I said to him, MITCHELL, *sit tight, be quiet!* We was just sittin up there, in circles, waitin to drop.

I preferred it up in the air, that's when I was most safe. See, When I was – up thar –

Up thar –

*(beat)*

Bah.

*(SARA busts into the kitchen and beelines towards the oven.)*

**SARA.** Shit – shit – shit –

**POP POP.** Bah –

**SARA.** Sorry, Pop Pop, I'm sorry, I don't usually say curse words –

**POP POP.** Whar's the baby?

**SARA.** *(loud)* Pop Pop – Lacey IS the baby. She grew UP.

*(She reaches for mitts and triumphantly rescues a burning casserole from the oven, then yells.)*

LACEY, GET IN HERE, HELP ME SET THE TABLE!

*(SARA guides POP POP by the elbow to the other side of the table.)*

SARA. I'm gonna put you on this side, cause we got a guest for dinner, okay? Is that okay?

*(She pushes down the brake on his chair, and returns to the fridge.)*

*(LACEY enters, running around the kitchen in a very short night shirt, wielding her broom gun in various broom gun wielding exercises.)*

Hay – HAY – you better help me! Put that thing down.

LACEY. I'm gonna, I can do both!

*(With one hand, she grabs a fistful of silverware and begins to plunk it down on the table, still wielding her gun.)*

SARA. Hay. HAY. Come here.

*(LACEY rolls her eyes, goes to her mom. Her mom frets with her hair.)*

SARA. Your hair's all messed up.

LACEY. I like it messed up!

SARA. Well I don't!

LACEY. It's not your hair, it's *my* hair!

SARA. Young lady, do *not* take that tone a voice with me, I swear –

LACEY. *(softer)* I have the right to my own hair.

*(She continues to set the table.)*

SARA. *(with no time to recover)* ABBY! Bring your friend in here, it's time to eat!

*(ABBY enters nervously, followed by CHIP. ABBY goes straight for a glass of wine, stopping momentarily to straighten POP POP's collar. CHIP stands in the doorway uncomfortably.)*

LACEY. Hay.

**CHIP.** Hay.

(to **SARAH**)

I do appreciate you havin me, I really do. You have a very nice house, like right outta a magazine.

**SARA.** Oh, stop! I like him! Aren't you sweet, you can come back anytime!

If I had known we were gonna have company, I woulda – the other night, I made my own Raviolis. From scratch. I like to make exotic foods for my family.

(Ashamed, she puts a big bottle of Wishbone Ranch on the table.)

The raviolis, they had ricotta cheese in it and truffle oil on top. You know how expensive truffle oil is? And it's just mushrooms!

**ABBY.** Come on, sit down, make yourself at home. It's not my home technically, but you can make yourself –at it – if you want.

(**CHIP** obliges, sits in a chair at the table, stiff. **POP POP** stares at him. Their eyes meet. **POP POP** nods at him.)

**POP POP.** OOHRAH!

**LACEY.** That's Pop Pop, he don't hear so good. He had a stroke, now he's demented.

**SARA.** (correcting her) He's got dementia. Only the beginnings though.

**POP POP.** I'm right here –

**LACEY.** He was in two wars, Korea AND Nam, his helicopter got shot down.

(**LACEY** kisses him on the cheek.)

**CHIP.** I'm very proud to meet you, Sir, it's an honor.

**POP POP.** I saw everything!

**CHIP.** Oh yeah, sounds like you did! What'd you see?

**LACEY.** He's got lots a good stories. Scary stories!

**POP POP.** The worst I ever saw – I tell you what – this was '52 –

(**POP** *tries to get out of his wheelchair.*)

**SARA.** Hay Pop – stay in there –

**POP POP.** DON'T NEED THIS CHAIR –

**SARA.** *(getting frustrated)* You're supposed to stay IN it.

**POP POP.** I'M A MAN –

**SARA.** I know, I didn't say you weren't, Damnit, Just stay in your chair, okay? Okay.

(**POP POP** *settles back into his chair – looking at* **CHIP**.)

**POP POP.** ….'52. *(studying* **CHIP***)* You're jes the right kind, the best kind! They was Marines there, good boys, the best boys. Wake Island, you heard? 'Don't fire til you see the whites in thar eyes –' Good story! You heard it?

**ABBY.** Pop, you're bein weird.

**POP POP.** Listen – you listen – I was up there in one a them Phantom 2's, in Rolling Thunder, we all got rolled out, ocean below. Cuttin through clouds, And when I was up thar –

*(Every one pauses to listen, feigning interest.)*

Up thar – I was – it was –

*(He is struggling.)*

I was –

*(He stops. It's gone.)*

**SARA.** That's nice, Pop Pop.

*(She sets a plate in front of him. He grabs her hand, squeezes it. He won't let it go.)*

Aw, aren't you sweet.

*(Gently, she pulls away.)*

**POP POP.** *(to* **CHIP***)* You a brave boy! Be proud, boy!

**CHIP.** Thank you sir.

**POP POP.** We – we gotta get the hell outta town! What is this place we are, eh?

*(He laughs.)*

**CHIP.** Alright, sir.

**ABBY.** Pop Pop, let's leave Chip alone, he's had a long day.

*(She tucks a napkin into his shirt.)*

**SARA.** Ab, is Chris not joinin us?

**ABBY.** No, he uh – he's workin late.

**POP POP.** Bah –

*(CHIP's eyes are on LACEY.)*

**CHIP.** What're you trying to do?

**LACEY.** Break down a door, duh!

**CHIP.** That's not how you do it.

**LACEY.** Yeah huh, I looked it up on the internet!

**CHIP.** Here, I'll show ya.

*(He takes the broom gun. He demonstrates the proper way to break down a door. It is swift and powerful. LACEY and ABBY watch in awe.)*

**LACEY.** COOL!

**SARA.** *(nervously)* I don't know where Ron is. RON!
Lacey, puts some pants on for Pete's sake.

**LACEY.** You ever broken down a real door before, like for real in a real situation?

**CHIP.** Sure have!

**LACEY.** Cool!

**ABBY.** *(loud)* One time, one time – there was the biggest roach ever in my kitchen, I took a lighter to it, lit it on fire, I watched it burn.

**SARA.** *(calling upstairs)* RON! DINNER'S ON THE TABLE! WE GOT COMPANY!

**LACEY.** I don't know how to do the hard stuff yet, but I been practicing. My daddy's gonna take me to the rifle range.

**SARA.** No, Lacey, he's not –

**LACEY.** He's a captain in the Army.

**POP POP.** I's never a good shot – better up thar – behind that wheel –

(*RON enters the kitchen, goes for a beer.* **CHIP** *stands immediately, nearly at attention, to greet him.*)

(*RON spots* **CHIP**.)

**RON.** Well, what's this? OohRah, Devil Dog!

(**CHIP** *stands immediately to greet him.*)

**CHIP.** (*smiling*) HUAHH, sir!

(*They shake hands.*)

It's very nice to meet you.

**RON.** What's a Marine doin in Fayetteville?

**CHIP.** (*quickly*) Special orders.

**RON.** That uniform's a bit much for this kitchen, though, Sure you don't wanna slip into something a little bit more comfortable?

**CHIP.** Nah, I like this just fine.

**SARA.** Pop Pop's here.

**RON.** How they treatin you in there? Pop?

**POP POP.** Mashed Potatoes! They got –

(*He trails off.*)

**RON.** Alright, then.

**LACEY.** DADDY LOOK!

(*She imitates what* **CHIP** *has taught her.*)

**ABBY.** Chip was on my flight. A Marine scared of flying, can you believe it?

**CHIP.** (*bellowing randomly*) I'm not SCARED –

**ABBY.** No, yeah – I know, I just – sorry. I was just talking.

(*to* **RON**)

He's due on base but it was so late already, so I just invited him for dinner.

I figured he could stay here tonight, he's got nowhere else to stay.

**LACEY.** He can sleep in my room!

(**SARA** *shoves utensils into* **LACEY**'s *hands.*)

**SARA.** Lacey. Hush.

ABBY. *(gazing at* CHIP, *but trying not to.)* He'll sleep in *my* room. And and and I'll sleep on the couch.

RON. Well, welcome.

*(They all sit.* SARA *begins to serve an odd looking casserole, heaping and steaming.* CHIP *eats hungrily.)*

CHIP. This is incredible, what is this?

SARA. *(proud)* It's got tater tots in it.

LACEY. My daddy just got back from over there, he's been four times on four tours.

SARA. He's getting out, though, he's done.

CHIP. Oh yeah?

LACEY. I'm gonna be in the army one day too one day or maybe probably a marine probably.

They don't let the girls do much now 'cept Intel, no offensive stuff, but I bet by the time I'm old enough things'll be different, what with Angelie Jolie and what with that crocodile hunter's daughter playing with snakes and girls bein all bad ass all the time and better than most boys.

SARA. Lacey, you're talking with your mouth full.

*(LACEY swallows.)*

LACEY. I think it's a fine idea, the Marine corps, because most people are shallow and horrible and stupid or at least most people in the ninth grade. I don't know, I'd rather not be that way. I wanna be able to take life into my own hands.

CHIP. I agree.

LACEY. You do?

CHIP. Sure do.

*(They smile at each other, with understanding.)*

CHIP. *(to* RON*)* How long you been in?

LACEY. MY Daddy was in since he was 18 years old cause he always felt called to no matter what, the feeling started when he was just round my age, a little younger, he's just using his God given skills.

**CHIP.** Me too.

> (**CHIP** *and* **RON** *meet eyes over dinner.*)

**CHIP.** You headed back over soon?

**RON.** I'm done with tours now.

**CHIP.** What're you gonna do?

**RON.** Stay home, focus on my family. Maybe get a boat.

**CHIP.** *(unimpressed)* Oh.

**SARA.** And a new dishwasher!

**LACEY.** And a tire swing!

**CHIP.** That all sounds real nice.

**RON.** Pop Pop, hand me that salad dressing.

> (**POP POP** *eats methodically.* **SARA** *passes the dressing over him to* **RON.** **CHIP** *has laid down his fork.*)

**CHIP.** Captain, you said?

> (**RON** *nods.*)

**CHIP.** You see any action while you were over there ?

**POP POP.** Over thar – the worst I saw – it was – '53, we were comin down low over the trees –

> (**RON** *wipes his mouth, clears his throat.*)

**RON.** I was doin strategy, getting convoys with supplies where they needed to go.

> (**CHIP** *nods, wanting something more and better.*)

**RON.** It was hot. Hotter this time than ever.

**CHIP.** That's what I hear.

> (*He squeezes* **SARA**'s *hand.*)

**RON.** Yep, just real happy to be back now, lookin forward to it.

**CHIP.** To what?

**SARA.** *(proudly)* He's gonna put down some carpet in the living room, is what he's gonna do!

**RON.** I am?

**SARA.** It's real easy, It makes the living room look real nice.

**RON.** Whatever you say, baby –

**SARA.** Also Ron might work for Krispy Kreme!

**CHIP.** *(laughing just a little)* You're gonna do what?

*(off everyone's look)*

…I'm sorry, that wasn't my place…..

**RON.** I'm not gonna do that.

*(**ABBY** stares at **CHIP**, lost.)*

**POP POP.** We were low – over the trees and – and –

**SARA.** Abby, you gonna eat something?

**ABBY.** What? Nah. I don't think I'm gonna eat anything ever again.

*(She smiles hungrily at **CHIP**.)*

## VII.

*(After dinner, RON stands at the sink. He picks up a dish.)*

RON. *(quietly, to himself)* Okay, I can do this.

*(He looks at a baking dish, still dirty. He scrubs at it. He scrubs at it, hard.)*

Goddamnit.

*(It slips out of his fingers. It plummets to the ground and breaks.)*

Goddamnit, goddamnit.

*(He picks up the pieces. CHIP approaches.)*

CHIP. You need help?

RON. What? Nah, thanks. I got this.

*(He deposits the glass pieces in the sink. CHIP watches him.)*

CHIP. So – What was it like over there really?

RON. I don't like to talk like that in fronta my family.

CHIP. Like what?

RON. About stuff I've done over there, or seen. You got a family?

CHIP. No.

RON. Well, when you do, you'll know what I mean.

CHIP. I sure would like to get over there, that's all.

*(RON looks out the window overlooking the backyard.)*

RON. You ever seen an acorn squash?

CHIP. What?

RON. It's a vegetable.

CHIP. I don't know –

RON. I got a garden back there, I grow squash in it. Or I'm going to, I tried to once, but this time I'm gonna do it for real. I'm gonna water the shit outta it and shit's gonna grow and I'm gonna make a salad.

*(He hands* CHIP *a dish to dry.)*

CHIP. Your little girl's something else.

RON. What's that supposed to mean?

CHIP. Nothin, just that she's something.

*(*CHIP *hands* RON *a dish to dry.)*

Just that you must be proud, you did good work with her.

RON. You think I forced that on her? She found that herself.

CHIP. Well, what you want her to be, a ballerina?

RON. Maybe like a writer or a teacher or a librarian –

CHIP. You WANT her to be a librarian?

RON. Something with her head.

CHIP. Is that what you're gonna do now, something with your head? You gonna go desk?

RON. What? Nah, something. Thinking of doing security or –

CHIP. I don't mean any disrespect, you just don't strike me as a desk type.

RON. I'm not, I just got a family to consider –

CHIP. So you're just gonna give up?

*(*RON *turns to him, studying him.)*

RON. I don't see it like that.

CHIP. No disrespect, sir.

RON. How long you been in?

CHIP. Oh, uh, not too long – see, the thing is –

RON. Cocky new green kid, I know your type, think you know everything. You been to Parris Island?

CHIP. Yeah.

RON. When were you there?

CHIP. *(quickly)* Two years back.

RON. Thought you said California.

CHIP. I was and / then I –

*(He takes a step closer.)*

RON. You a US Marine?

*(**CHIP** is quiet. **RON** takes a closer look at his uniform. Sees the pants are too short [or too long.])*

RON. What the fuck is this, Halloween?

CHIP. Not that I know of, sir –

RON. You a US Marine?

CHIP. Sort of –

RON. What are you doin with that uniform if you are *sort of* a Marine?

CHIP. Buddy in basic, I was on my way out and it was layin on his bunk and I wanted so bad to put it on me, so I did and I couldn't take it off, I just couldn't, it just felt too good, you know? You ever put yours on just for sport? You know what I mean?

I didn't mean any harm –

RON. *(hard)* Impersonating a military officer is a crime, you know that right?

CHIP. I GOT ASTHMA.

*(Pause. This was super hard for him to say.)*

I got fuckin asthma. I didn't tell em, They found out, they kicked me out.

RON. Who gives a shit, you didn't *earn* those blues!

CHIP. I almost did. I made it real far. In boot camp.

RON. What, am I supposed to tell you good job?

CHIP. I made it to the gas chambers, sir.

RON. Quit callin me sir.

CHIP. I just got a lotta respect for you, okay?

RON. Gas chamber's week eight, You got through eight weeks? With asthma?

CHIP. I had it my whole life, I'm used to it.

RON. You can't just go around in a uniform you didn't earn!

CHIP. I *am* a Marine. I just *am*.

> I tried college, I tried that. Felt outta place, why would I wanna be where I can't use my skills? So I enlisted. All through basic, I was the best and they *knew* it, too. They saw how good I was, how bad I wanted it.
>
> It wasn't til the tear gas, sir, I could hide it til then. They found me, they say I was dead for a minute.
>
> Yeah when they pulled me out. Came back to life, though.
>
> *(beat)*
>
> You may think I'm weak but I got a heart like a stone I swear to God.

RON. If they kicked you out, you're out.

CHIP. You don't know, man. Sir.

RON. Oh, what don't I know?

CHIP. What it feels like to have somebody tell you you can't do the one thing you gotta do.

RON. Actually I do, actually.

*(a small moment of understanding)*

RON. Well what're you doin in Fayetteville?

CHIP. Just heard stuff, bout here. Bout the way people are here.

RON. Like what?

CHIP. Supportive, I guess? The town where a base is's gotta be supportive, or at least have an energy that's – I thought maybe – I could try and get back in. Maybe the Army.

RON. What, you don't see it as a downgrade?

CHIP. I see it as service.

RON. You're one cocky devil dog, Chip.

CHIP. Yessir.

RON. You think Army's got lower standards?

CHIP. DIFFERENT standards –

RON. Oh, You think we'll take just anybody?

**CHIP.** I never said that.

**RON.** Same thing's gonna happen, why put yourself through that? If you can't cut it, you can't cut it.

**CHIP.** I just – I just gotta try. I gotta do *something*. I feel so useless! How'm I supposed to fall asleep at night when I haven't done anything worthwhile all goddamn day? I just lay there and I know I haven't done nothing all day, my day was nothing.

This is what I'm supposed to be doing.

I was thinking – maybe – you bein a captain – maybe you could – maybe there's somebody you could talk to for me –

**RON.** I don't think so.

*(He heads for the stairs.)*

**RON.** Take that uniform off, it ain't yours. If anyone ever asks, you weren't here in my kitchen, understood? UNDERSTOOD?

*(CHIP nods.)*

And I suggest you be gone before I wake up.

*(RON is gone. CHIP stands alone in the kitchen. Slowly, he begins to unbutton his coat, starting at his throat. He releases a huge breath of air.)*

## VII.

*(The guest bedroom where* **ABBY** *has been staying.* **CHIP** *is in his wifebeater, sitting on the edge of a fluffy day bed, removing his boots.)*

*(***ABBY*** watches him from the doorway. She has another glass of wine.)*

**ABBY.** Nothing like the sight of a man taking off his blues.

**CHIP.** *(startled)* Hey.

**ABBY.** Hey. You need anything? There's towels there in the closet if you wanna take a shower or anything. You wanna take a shower?

**CHIP.** Probably will in the morning.

**ABBY.** You could take one now if you wanted to.

**CHIP.** Pretty beat.

**ABBY.** There's soap in there and I found you a toothbrush.

*(pause)*

You wanna do a shot?

**CHIP.** What?

**ABBY.** You wanna do a shot of whiskey?

**CHIP.** Not right now.

**ABBY.** Okay, well.

*(pause)*

I don't really love him. Christopher. I mean I do, but I don't. You ever been in that situation?

**CHIP.** Not that I can recall. Only people I loved ever, I really loved them.

**ABBY.** Well, it's hard, just so you know. It's a hard situation to be in.

*(***CHIP*** nods politely.)*

When's the last time you had a girlfriend?

**CHIP.** Bout two years ago.

**ABBY.** What was her name?

**CHIP.** Jennifer.

**ABBY.** When was the last time you had – had a girl? Just in general.

(**CHIP** *blushes.*)

**CHIP.** Nah, I don't know.

(**ABBY** *takes a step into the room, shutting the door behind her.*)

**ABBY.** Can I talk to you about something?

**CHIP.** I'm pretty tired.

**ABBY.** It's pretty important.

**CHIP.** Alright. What you want to talk about?

**ABBY.** Lust.

**CHIP.** Lust?

**ABBY.** Yeah, lust, you ever heard of it?

**CHIP.** Yeah.

(*She sits down next to him on the bed.*)

**ABBY.** I really liked talking to you on the plane. I feel like we had a real good conversation, one of the best I've had in a long time.

**CHIP.** We did.

**ABBY.** I'm not wearing any underwear.

(**CHIP** *shifts uncomfortably. He has no idea what to do with her advances – and doesn't seem that into her at all.*)

**CHIP.** Listen / I –

**ABBY.** No, you listen instead. You don't have to say anything. I'm not asking for anything from you.

**CHIP.** I got a lot on my mind – I'm not really looking to – Eye on the prize, that's kinda how I am.

**ABBY.** There are other, smaller, more special prizes.

**CHIP.** Yeah but I kinda gotta keep my focus on the one.

**ABBY.** I know, and I'm not askin you for much. Listen. I only ever felt lust just a few times in my life. I think it's the most wonderful feeling in the world, and when I find it, I gotta grab it. Please, I just – could I just – do something for you?

**CHIP.** Do something?

**ABBY.** Yeah, do something to you. All you have to do is lay back.

*(She is near tears.)*

Listen. I don't get it very often, I just – just close your eyes.

I just – I really need –

Aren't you lonely?

**CHIP.** Not especially.

**ABBY.** Don't you at least want me, or it?

*(She takes a hand tentatively to his face. He closes his eyes. He leans back.)*

**CHIP.** Door locked?

*(**ABBY** nods.)*

*(**CHRISTOPHER** appears in his room at home, in front of a mirror in a wife beater. He flexes. It's sad.)*

*(She unzips **CHIP**'s pants. She turns out the light.)*

*(**CHRISTOPHER** remains.)*

**CHRISTOPHER.** Abby, I – *(He clears his throat.)* I marry you. Because I want to, because from the moment I saw you, I knew you were so – so, it. No.

Abby, I marry you, because, you know, I'm a relationship guy, and you're it. Because –

Because I like sleeping next to you, you're like a pillow. You're like a Swiss cake roll, you're –

No.

Abby, I take you as my wife, like, for a very very very long time, well into our fifties, because you make me feel – you make me feel – *you make me feel like a natural...*

Eh.

I take you as my wife because I love you. And I know this because pretty much everything I do – *I do it for you – dang*it.

**CHRISTOPHER.** *(cont.)* I'm pretty excited, on this day, in which I get to make you mine, legitimately.

Gonna stick that ring on your finger. Yay....

Because I love you because, just as you are. I don't want you to be anyone else but you.

I accept your weaknesses and encourage your strengths. Also, you have the most spectacular hair on your head.

I think also, pretty much, I just love you because when I met you, I needed you, and you were it. *Are* it, so.

That's pretty much why I love you. And if you want to know how much, It's a lot.

*(He likes this, so he writes this down.)*

I take you as my wife.

*(Lights fade on him.)*

# ACT II

## I.

*(The next morning, the kitchen.)*

*(SARA is taking wine glasses out of their Target boxes, lining them up neatly on the table.)*

*(ABBY walks in, fresh from sleep, with a huge smile on her face. She goes for coffee.)*

**SARA.** *(not looking at her)* Chris's called three times just this morning.

**ABBY.** I'll see him later, we're going to look at pillows or something. *(She sits at the table.)* Where's Lacey?

**SARA.** She went to Home Depot with Ron, he's getting stuff for the living room carpet. And maybe lookin at a new dishwasher for me. And maybe a ficus plant for the hall. He's doin real well, Ron is.

Your new friend was gone before I even woke up.

*(ABBY smiles, hard, into her coffee. SARA sees this.)*

**SARA.** What the hell are you smiling like that for?

**ABBY.** Nothing.

*(ABBY looks at the wine glasses.)*

**SARA.** *(proudly)* They're for Lacey's party Sunday. Ron got em, he got up early this morning and went to Target and got all sorts of stuff for the house.

**ABBY.** So you're gonna get the kids drunk?

**SARA.** For the PARENTS.

That one's for white wine, and these're for red, and these're for sherry which I think is dessert wine. They're just like the ones they use in Tuscany like in *Under the Tuscan Sun.*

**SARA.** *(cont.)* You hold em at the base and swish it around and the wine breathes, cause apparently wine's gotta breathe too.

**ABBY.** Since when do you drink wine?

**SARA.** I don't know. Since I want a complete kitchen, and the / parents –

**ABBY.** Alright.

**SARA.** And for dinner parties.

**ABBY.** Since when do you have dinner parties?

**SARA.** I'm waitin til my kitchen's complete, Damn!

**ABBY.** Okay, okay! Geez louise. Not sleep good?

**SARA.** I slept fine, did you?

**ABBY.** Yeah.

**SARA.** On the couch? The whole night?

**ABBY.** Yeah, on the couch.

**SARA.** Ron thinks it best that you go on and find yourself your own place to live. Me, I don't care, I don't mind, I like havin you here but Ron –

**ABBY.** Wait – what?

**SARA.** I mean, it's not the biggest house in the world – walls're thin, and we need our privacy, you know? I'm only in my middle thirties and I have – sexual – needs, and so does Ron.

**ABBY.** So because he says so, I gotta go?

**SARA.** Not JUST / because –

**ABBY.** You always do whatever he wants!

**SARA.** You just shouldn't have done that in my *house*, Abby. This is *my* house. I don't want Lacey bein around that stuff.

**ABBY.** What stuff?

**SARA.** Just – Why don't you just move in with Christopher?

**ABBY.** Cause, cause, we're getting married, and then we'll get our own place. His place nows' too small and his underwear is everywhere. I don't, I'm not *ready* for that, okay?

SARA. *Are* you getting married?

ABBY. What do you mean, *are* we getting married?

SARA. The walls're here are thin, Abby. *Thin.*

What'd you do last night?

Heard you, what were you doing?

*(pause)*

ABBY. Exercises.

SARA. Uh huh. You just best be careful, Abby, cause marriage is sacred.

*(SARA begins setting the glasses on a shelf.)*

I just think it's best you find some place, til the wedding.

ABBY. We'll see, yeah.

SARA. I mean it. I'm like *real* serious right now.

ABBY. Okay.

*(Pause. ABBY picks up a wine glass, inspects it.)*

ABBY. They're not even real glass.

*(SARA grabs it from her.)*

SARA. They're a thick durable PLASTIC so they break less. It's what Martha freakin STEWART said to do so just lay off, you wanna tell her she's wrong?

ABBY. She *did* go to jail.

SARA. She's a good lady, everybody makes mistakes!

ABBY. It's just kinda white trash.

SARA. Excuse me, *What?*

ABBY. Nothin.

*(SARA begins putting the glasses away, pissed. She stops.)*

SARA. If I'm so white trash then what're you?

ABBY. I am – I am *not* –

SARA. You coulda gone other places, Abby, you didn't have to stay here, you're always / bitchin –

ABBY. I didn't have any *money* to go any places.

SARA. Where there's a will, there's a way!

**ABBY.** And what about you?

**SARA.** I never had any will!

(*pause*)

Hell, I don't care. You see this house? This house is fulla nice things.

**ABBY.** Rental.

**SARA.** Rent to OWN. You know how much money Ron makes a year? Sixty. Sixty THOUSAND.
How much *you* make?

**ABBY.** How much do YOU make?

**SARA.** I make my FAMILY.

(*She throws a wine glass. It bounces. They look at it. They don't know what to do so they laugh. Both are still hurt.* **SARA** *picks it up. The puts it gently on the shelf.*)

(**SARA** *stacks the glasses.*)

**SARA.** My daughter's a little boy. She's not supposed to be like that, she's supposed to be like *me*, like mother like daughter.

(*She sits at the table.*)

**SARA.** What's that crap you drink, the Zinfandel?

**ABBY.** White Zinfandel, yeah.

**SARA.** I'm gonna have a glass a that.

**ABBY.** It's nine am.

**SARA.** Yeah, well, it's my kitchen and I do what I want.

## II.

*(Later that morning.)*

*(**ABBY** and **CHRISTOPHER** are at Bed Bath and Beyond perusing duvet covers. **ABBY** is bored and distracted. She sips a Venti frozen fat thing. They are pushing a cart full of bedding.)*

**CHRISTOPHER.** This is squishy, yeah, I like this. It's *super* soft. I could totally tap that *ass* on this.

**ABBY.** Yeah.

**CHRISTOPHER.** You like the color?

**ABBY.** Yeah, its good.

**CHRISTOPHER.** Or how bout something with like *dragons* on it. I'm kidding, I'm kidding, you shoulda seen your face. No, I like this. You think it's too – what color is this?

**ABBY.** *(bored)* It's a purple.

**CHRISTOPHER.** Is that gay? I guess it's definitely not gay cause we'll be married, and you're a lady. *My* lady.

**ABBY.** It's kind of – mauve.

**CHRISTOPHER.** Mauve and purple are not even REMOTELY related, I bet you twenty bucks.

*(He whips out his iPhone, types this in. Pause. Hand on his hip, he watches his phone.)*

It's loading.

*(Pause. It loads.)*

AH– oh. You're right.

*(He picks up a pillow in a sham. Sings – )*

*A whole new bed –*

*(She's not laughing.)*

**CHRISTOPHER.** So what happened with that Marine guy?

**ABBY.** What?

**CHRISTOPHER.** Did he get to the base?

**ABBY.** Yeah, he came over for dinner, then yeah, he went to the base.

**CHRISTOPHER.** Oh. *(beat)* I want you to get whatever you want, I leave it totally up to you. I mean, if you want like Care Bears, I gotta draw a line. You want Care Bears, Ab?

*(She smiles and shakes her head, picking a stray string off the duvet.)*

Well then um – what do you want?

*(**ABBY** considers what to say.)*

You okay, or – ?

**ABBY.** Kinda tired, kinda stressed out.

*(She sees his face. She smiles at him.)*

Love you though.

**CHRISTOPHER.** *(loud, with a weird voice)* You sure cause when I kissed you this morning you had some other nigger's dick on your breath!

*(Pause. Color drains from **ABBY**'s face. He very obviously has no idea why he said this.)*

**ABBY.** …What?

**CHRISTOPHER.** Oh – uh – sorry – I heard that on, um, Comedy Central this morning, um, dot com. I thought it was funny.

**ABBY.** What the fuck? You're – you're *gross*.

**CHRISTOPHER.** You love it!

*(He pushes her back onto the bed playfully, trying to be sexy, tries to kiss her, but she moves and he kind of falls off. He climbs back onto the fake bed.)*

**CHRISTOPHER.** PDA. So.

**ABBY.** You seriously think that?

**CHRISTOPHER.** What?

**ABBY.** Do you seriously think that I would – with somebody else?

**CHRISTOPHER.** No, not really.

**ABBY.** Why not?

**CHRISTOPHER.** You just wouldn't do that. It's contrary to your nature, you're like the best person I know.

**ABBY.** Yeah, I know.

*(He kisses her.)*

**CHRISTOPHER.** Grrr I wanna cuddle you forever. Let's never go home. Let's Live Here.

*(He holds her. Her eyes are wide with the potential of wonderfully bad things.)*

### III.

*(The Rifle Range, outside, day.)*

*(***LACEY*** *is shooting like a pro, with ear guards on.* ***RON****is supervising, holding a gun. His guards are around his neck.* ***CHIP*** *approaches, watches* ***RON*** *watching his daughter. In short shorts and a large wife beater, she is young and muscular, a little lady GI JOE.)*

**CHIP.** Hey.

**RON.** Hey.

> *(beat)*

Where's your costume?

**CHIP.** Took it off, for now.

> *(They watch* ***LACEY*** *shoot.)*

**CHIP.** Damn. She's good.

**RON.** I know.

> *(Beat. They watch her shoot.)*

**CHIP.** I talked to a recruiter.

**RON.** Oh yeah?

**CHIP.** Yeah.

> *(beat)*

Figured I'd be honest with him.

**RON.** Yeah, how'd that go?

**CHIP.** He said no.

**RON.** I figured.

**CHIP.** What he doesn't know is I don't give up that easy.

**RON.** I can see that.

Listen, Chip, how bout this –

find a nice girl and buy a house. Get a dog and a savings account.

**CHIP.** Don't seem to work for you, why would it work for me?

> *(beat)*

**RON.** Go on home, Chip.

**CHIP.** I don't have a home.

**RON.** Go make one.

**CHIP.** I gotta lot a respect for you, Ron, don't think that I don't.

(**RON** *smiles wryly, liking the sound of this.*)

**CHIP.** That recruiter.

**RON.** What about him?

**CHIP.** He had a boss. A higher up.

**RON.** So?

**CHIP.** Maybe if, maybe you could talk to him. Just tell him about me, tell him about how far I got, how good I am, how bad I – if you could just *try* –

**RON.** Chip –

**CHIP.** Listen, I got just what you're lookin for.

I'm a good shot. I'm loyal, like a good dog. Faithful, I say my prayers. Yeah cause I believe in God, barely anybody will admit that anymore but I do. I can feel him workin in me and pointing me this way, to serve this country. This country been like a dad to me.

(*beat*)

**RON.** Those were some real nice words, Chip.

Thing is, there's nothing left.

**CHIP.** What?

**RON.** There's nothing left to do over there.

**CHIP.** That's not true.

**RON.** It is. Apparently they don't need us anymore. We're all comin back.

**CHIP.** There's stuff goin on, there's always stuff going on –

**RON.** Take my word. Anybody who's over there is just trainin the new police. Playin card games, accidentally settin flares off and lightin their on pants on fire.

They got burger kings and pizza huts and swimming pools on base. Haji shops with Ben Stiller movies, fake ray bans. Grunts shootin each other through the ankles on accident, friendly fire.

**RON.** (cont) You assemble a raid, you wake a family up, middle of the night, they're smuggling cigarettes. It's cigarettes you find there, it's no weapons, no IED's. And they laugh at you.

**CHIP.** Well what about Afghanistan?

**RON.** They just sent over 5,000 from Lejeune son, we missed that boat.

Just drop it Chip, you best focus on something else.

**CHIP.** Well, what about here?

Like those gas tanks on I-40? I read about em, listed as one of the most vulnerable targets on the east coast. saw em from the plane when I was flyin in. Miles and miles of em. Somebody could bust in on that, blow that up. Or we could stop em.

**RON.** You really think that?

**CHIP.** I'm just sayin, something like that. That'd feel good.

**RON.** What do you want, a medal?

**CHIP.** Yeah.

You're really telling me there's *nothing* left / to do over there?

**RON.** Not really, son, not right now. They got everybody they need.

**CHIP.** Well – what're we supposed to do, then?

(**RON** *hesitates.*)

**RON.** It's better at home.

**CHIP.** Is it?

(*beat*)

**RON.** Yes.

I'm stayin put, now. Sara wants me to – carpets. In the living room, I can do that. A swing set for Lacey, hell, she's too old for that now, maybe I'll dig us a pool, hell, I don't know, I'll install a security system, I'll – I'll do *something*.

(**RON** *trails off.*)

**CHIP.** So you think you could – talk to someone for me?

**RON.** Chip –

**CHIP.** PLEASE.

*(beat)*

**RON.** I'll see what I can do, okay?

**CHIP.** Thank you, Sir.

*(pointing to gun)*

That yours?

**RON.** Nah, it stays on base.

**CHIP.** You got your own?

**RON.** Yeah, got quite a collection back at the house.

**CHIP.** You wanna shoot later? I bet you twenty bucks I'm a better shot.

**RON.** Forty.

**CHIP.** Alright, you're on!

*(beat)*

**RON.** Nah, can't today. I got an interview.

**CHIP.** Oh yeah, for what?

*(beat)*

**RON.** At the Home Depot.

Don't look at me like that. They need a manager. It's a good job, I like home stuff, I know a lot about it. Plus I took some business classes on base.

**CHIP.** No, I'm sure it's a great opportunity.

**RON.** It is.

**CHIP.** Maybe we can shoot some other time then –

**RON.** Nah, Sara doesn't like me ta –

**CHIP.** You always do what she says?

*(**RON** takes this in. Moves towards **LACEY**.)*

**RON.** Lacey, that's enough for today.

*(**LACEY** doesn't hear him. She shoots.)*

LACEY, I SAID THAT'S ENOUGH.

*(He grabs the barrel of her gun. She turns it quickly towards him, instinctively.)*

*(She pulls the ear guards off her ears, lowers the gun.)*

**LACEY.** Damn, okay.

**RON.** I said that's *enough* for today.

*(**LACEY** puts down the gun.)*

I gotta get going. Lacey, Aunt Abby's gonna come get you and give you a ride home, you stay put. I'll see you back at the house.

*(He goes.)*

**LACEY.** I'm a better shot than most of all the men and he don't even say so, he could at least say so. I don't get it, why don't I make him proud?

**CHIP.** He seems like a tough one to crack.

**LACEY.** You have no idea.

*(She aims to shoot again.)*

**CHIP.** You're not so bad.

**LACEY.** What'd you mean, not so bad?

**CHIP.** *(teasing)* Yeah, you're pretty good, you're alright.

**LACEY.** Well maybe not as good as YOU but you're bigger than me.

**CHIP.** Yeah, you're pretty small, you're just a little thing.

**LACEY.** I'm not THAT small.

**CHIP.** You're good, okay?

**LACEY.** Really, you think so?

*(**CHIP** nods. She smiles.)*

**LACEY.** Thanks.

**CHIP.** Your form's a little off.

**LACEY.** *(determined.)* Show me, then.

**CHIP.** Nah, I don't show and tell.

**LACEY.** Come on, if you're so much better than me, show me.

*(Pause. **CHIP** spits.)*

**CHIP.** Okay, fine. First you hold your gun like a girl.

**LACEY.** I DO NOT!

**CHIP.** No, not *you,* damn, I mean – that's how you're *supposed* to. Hard and soft at the same time.

**LACEY.** I don't know what that means.

**CHIP.** What, you never been held like that?

**LACEY.** No.

**CHIP.** Here. Pick it up.

*(She picks it up, focused.)*

No, nah.

*(He goes behind her, putting his hands onto her hands, moving them.)*

**CHIP.** Yeah, like –

**LACEY.** Yeah – Oh.

**CHIP.** See?

*(**ABBY** appears holding yet another Venti surgary coffee thing. Her face falls when she sees this. **LACEY** is mildly oblivious to his touch.)*

**LACEY.** Yeah, that's better.

**CHIP.** Feel the difference?

**LACEY.** Yeah, I do! Feels better, feels more natural! Wow, that is awesome – where'd you learn that, the Marines teach you that?

*(**CHIP** smiles, feeling warm and needed.)*

**CHIP.** Taught myself in my backyard.

**LACEY.** Me too –

**CHIP.** Other kids playin capture the flag, makin out in rose bushes, ridin bikes to the gas station, I'm outside with my BB gun –

**LACEY.** Me too!

**ABBY.** HI!

*(**CHIP** drops his hands.)*

They got a drive through at the Starbucks!

**LACEY.** Aunt Abby, Chip's perfecting my hold! Check this out!

*(She shows* **AUNT ABBY**, *who smiles.)*

**ABBY.** I um, I brought you coffee! Well it's coffee, sort of. It's got whipped crème on it.

**CHIP.** Thanks, but I don't drink coffee.

**ABBY.** ….Oh.

**LACEY.** I'll take it!

*(She takes it happily, slurps. She burps loud, giggles,* **CHIP** *laughs.)*

**ABBY.** You sleep okay?

*(***CHIP*** nods quickly, embarrassed.)*

**CHIP.** Yeah yeah yeah –

**ABBY.** *(expectant)* Great, me too. Wow, look at you, you're all sweaty.

*(pause)*

**CHIP.** Well / I gotta

**ABBY.** Maybe / later you could

**ABBY.** You need a place to stay again tonight?

**CHIP.** Nah, I can stay here on base, they got rooms.

**ABBY.** Oh, yeah, okay, but just in case, if you / ever –

**CHIP.** Yeah –

**ABBY.** You know where I live!

**CHIP.** I sure do.

*(He starts to go.)*

**LACEY.** Hay you wanna come to my birthday party tomorrow?

**ABBY.** Lacey, Chip's gotta focus on his training now –

**CHIP.** I love birthday parties.

**LACEY.** There aren't gonna be a lot of kids there, mainly grown ups. Mainly just an excuse for my mom to have people over to the house. It's gonna suck but maybe you'll like it.

**CHIP.** Round what time?

**LACEY.** Round 2.

**CHIP.** I'll see you then.

(*He goes.*)

**ABBY.** (*after him*) I could pick you up if –

(*He's gone.* **LACEY** *is re-tying her boots.* **ABBY** *watches her body, spitefully.*)

**LACEY.** Chip's so cool, he's like the coolest person ever.

(*pause*)

**ABBY.** Boys don't like boygirls.

**LACEY.** What?

**ABBY.** You're getting real good at shooting, huh?

**LACEY.** Yeah.

**ABBY.** You like boys?

**LACEY.** What? No. I mean yeah, but not really right now.

(*pause*)

**ABBY.** Spending a lotta time with your Dad.

**LACEY.** He just got back!

**ABBY.** Maybe your Mom's getting sad.

**LACEY.** What?

**ABBY.** Nothin.

I'm just sayin, maybe your Mom's getting sad cause there's nothing you want to do with her.

**LACEY.** (*hurt*) I do LOTS with her.

**ABBY.** If you don't do any girl things, if you aren't girly, what you going to do with your mom?

**LACEY.** Why're you bein mean to me?

**ABBY.** I'm not bein mean.

Come on. I'll take you home.

(**ABBY** *goes.* **LACEY** *follows after her, desolate.*)

## V.

*(Sunday, the next day. The birthday party. It's the day of the show, ya'll.)*

*(Sounds of the party, and the people who are forced to be there, spill in from the deck. **POP POP** sits by himself at the table in his wheelchair, wearing a party hat.)*

**POP POP.** We gonna eat yet? It's past my dinner time! It's time to eat!
Hello?

*(He settles.)*

Birthday parties're little wars! All the business, all the nonsense, all the protocol.

I missed mosta them. Did Grams ever tell ya?

I missed your ma's. Year and year again.

Your grams, she couldn't take it.

See, The first time I gone, she said – *Don't go.* I say *I gotta.* She say, *I be waitin by the door with the screen door shut so the flies don't get in.*

So – so when I was up thar – when I come flyin down, I thought –

Is she waitin by the door *right now?*

I missed all the parties.

*(He tries to pull the hat off, but he can't.)*

*(**ABBY** moves into the kitchen and heads towards the kitchen table. She is wearing the predictable Bohemian halter dress of a Target patron.)*

**POP POP.** Whar's the baby?

**ABBY.** The baby *is* Lacey, she grew up.

**POP POP.** You bring any candy? Your grams, she had candy – little candies –

**ABBY.** How do I look? It's party time, huh?

*(She tenderly straightens his shirt.)*

**POP POP.** *(holding her by the wrist)* That boy out thar, you be good to him, that boy –

**ABBY.** What, Christopher?

**POP POP.** That boy loves you – he ain't no soldier but he a good boy, good boy for you –

**ABBY.** I *know.*

Look at you, all messed up. There you go, you look real nice. You got mustard on your nose, hold on.

*(She wipes it off.)*

There ya go. If grandma were here, she'd be all over you, you look hot, look at you. She's watchin you right now, I bet she's like *damn.*

**POP POP.** I'S SUPPOSED TO DIE FIRST.

**ABBY.** I know –

**POP POP.** WHAR'D SHE GO?

**ABBY.** Some kind of better place.

**POP POP.** She was waitin by the door – when I come flyin down –

*(**ABBY** goes back to the table, absently arranging something on a tray.)*

**POP POP.** Hrmph.

*(**CHRISTOPHER** enters, wearing an apron, holding a spatula.)*

**ABBY.** Grill ready?

**CHRISTOPHER.** Embarrassing, wow –

**ABBY.** What?

**CHRISTOPHER.** So *how* do I light it?

**ABBY.** Are you serious?

**CHRISTOPHER.** I mean I consider myself to be a smart guy, but the coals are just NOT turning gray, and, I've been waiting like PATIENTLY – I'm supposed to wait for this, right? – and I'm starting to get very self-conscious cause people are staring at the pile of cold meat next to me sort of sitting there, being cold, so. Is there like some sort of ancient man trick or am / I just –

**ABBY.** You can't even – YOU JUST MAKE IT BURN, CHRIS, YOU JUST MAKE IT HOT, OKAY?

*(Pause. **CHRISTOPHER**, red, hurt, retreats.)*

**CHRISTOPHER.** Yeah – so – okay – I'm just going to do that.

*(He leaves. **ABBY** puts her head in her hands. **SARA** buzzes into the kitchen in an equally predictable party dress. **RON** follows her in a nice polo shirt, carrying a cake box.)*

**SARA.** Yeah, just set that on the counter.

HOLY CRAP I GOTTA PUT THE DIP IN THE MICRO-WAVE!!

**RON.** Baby –

**SARA.** *(hot)* Don't you even try to talk to me right now.

**RON.** What the hell's wrong?

**SARA.** You didn't finish the floors, they look terrible and EVERYBODY's judging me right now!

**RON.** I *tried* –

**SARA.** Tried? You spend all your time on base and you tell me you *tried*?

Abby, what're you doing?

**ABBY.** Helping.

**SARA.** How're you helping?

**ABBY.** I'm putting things on *plates.*

*(**SARA** reaches for the dip.)*

**SARA.** Everybody's wondering when the burger's are gonna be ready, everybody's hungry. Why'd we let Chris do the grill? Ron, go do the grill.

**ABBY.** Chris can do it.

**RON.** That kid couldn't light a match.

**ABBY.** So?

**SARA.** Ron, be sweet. Abby – go help him.

**ABBY.** Don't want to.

**SARA.** Okay fine, then put these napkins on the corner a the table by the basil plant.

**ABBY.** You have a basil plant?

**SARA.** Just put em on the table!! And fan em out! Stack them and fan them!!!

(**ABBY** *goes.*)

**SARA.** You're getting food on your new shirt, put this on.

*(She grabs a floral apron.)*

**RON.** I'm not putting that on, they're people here.

**SARA.** Just for a MINUTE, damn!

*(She tries to put it on him. He resists, for a second, nearly violently. He stops. He takes it from her. He puts it on.* **SARA** *continues to bustle around the kitchen.)*

Think I can just microwave this? Ron? It says to micro-wave it, I guess it's just a dip. Will you hand me the parmesan cheese? You shake it on top. You're sup-posed to use the real stuff I think, the real stuff would be better but hell, nobody's perfect.

Remind me to stir it in a minute or it'll be cold in the middle. Okay. What next.

Don't just sit there, help me please?

**RON.** Settle down, Sara –

**SARA.** I will NOT.

Put the candles in the cake but don't let Lacey see. Put 14 candles, put 13 around the outside and one in the middle but don't let her see it. Make sure somebody gets a picture when she sees it, I want to get her face.

We gotta get a family picture, too, don't let me forget.

**RON.** That sounds nice.

**SARA.** Where did I put the tortilla chips? There's two bags out there and was supposed to be one more. Should I fill the bowl out there yet? I guess people just got here. Is it weird that the adults are drinking, I mean, is that weird for Lacey and her friends, is that a bad influence, is that weird? Regina's had one glass a wine, I gotta keep my eye on her, make sure she doesn't take her shirt off. That'd be quite the party.

*(Finally, a moment of silence. She turns, looks at* **RON***, square.)*

**RON.** ....What?

**SARA.** I heard you digging around in the garage last night.

**RON.** I was looking for something.

**SARA.** Your guns?

*(pause)*

**RON.** Yeah.

**SARA.** I moved them.

**RON.** Why?

**SARA.** Why you want them?

**RON.** Just do.

**SARA.** Why?

**RON.** Where'd you put them?

**SARA.** I wanna know why you want them first.

**RON.** THEY'RE NOT YOUR FUCKIN PROPERTY.

**SARA.** Okay, okay, they're back in the shed!

*(beat)*

Please don't yell like that, not while there're people here....

*(She grabs a tray outta the oven. It's got little hot dogs on it. She stares at it, desperately sad.)*

Are we white trash?

**RON.** What?

**SARA.** If this party doesn't go right I might kill myself.

**RON.** It's going fine.

**SARA.** It's NOT. HELP ME.

**RON.** I'm TRYING.

**SARA.** You're NOT TRYIN HARD ENOUGH.

You said you were gonna stay home this time, you PROMISED.

You said we were gonna have PICTURES AND TRIPS.

**RON.** We still can have that stuff, baby – I just gotta – first – JUST GIMMEE A MINUTE –

**SARA.** *(starting to lose it)* I made this home nice for you, I picked everything out, you don't think it's nice?

**RON.** I love this house!

**SARA.** You *hate* it!

**RON.** It kinda makes me feel like I can't breathe, okay, like you're sittin on my chest!

**SARA.** You're gonna kill me one day!

**RON.** ...*What?*

**SARA.** You're gonna shoot me and it's gonna hurt!

**RON.** Baby, I would never shoot you!

**SARA.** Promise you'll never shoot me.

**RON.** Promise.

**POP POP.** No point in fightin! yellin is empty! It won't matter, fifty years from now!

**SARA.** Am I not enough for you anymore?

**RON.** I didn't know you used to be –

**SARA.** WHAT?

**RON.** Damnit, that's not what I meant –

**SARA.** Or maybe you're not enough for *me* anymore. Maybe that's it. You're supposed to be so big and so brave but you're scared a me, scared a Lacey, running off on me every chance you get, what is it, you don't wanna be here with me? You don't wanna take care of me?

**RON.** *(quietly)* Fuck you Sara –

**SARA.** Fuck ME, Ron? Fuck YOU with a stick!

*(ABBY returns into the kitchen, entering the moment.*
*SARA turns away, drying her eyes, smoothing her dress.)*

**ABBY.** People'll are starting to wonder where Lacey is.

**SARA.** She'll be down. And Ron, you're gonna escort her in, I'm gonna put some music on, and you're gonna escort her in, and then you guys are gonna dance together.

**RON.** Dance?

**SARA.** Yeah, the father-daughter slow dance, I already told you about it!

(**RON** *obviously hates this.*)

**POP POP.** Bah.

(*He pulls at his hat.*)

**SARA.** Ron, get that hat offa him.

(**LACEY** *comes down stairs in a pink party dress, hair in a high ponytail, tiara in place. She looks miserable. Beneath the dress, combat boots.*)

(*Everyone stares. Beat.*)

**POP POP.** You got any candy?

**SARA.** Sweetie – Oh my God – you / look –

**RON.** Well, look at you!

**POP POP.** The baby grow up!

(**CHIP** *enters in a nice polo tucked into baggy jeans.*)

**CHIP.** Hey, everyone, sorry / I'm –

(*He spots* **LACEY.**)

Whoa, what you wearin that for?

(**LACEY** *turns red. She runs upstairs. Pause.*)

Uh – was that out loud?

**SARA.** LACEY! GET BACK DOWN HERE, YOU LIKE NICE, YOU LOOK SO NICE!
WE GOTTA TAKE THE FAMILY PICTURE! Chip, I'm real glad you're here, will you take it?
Where's the camera? Aw hell, where's my digital camera? Should we take one of everybody? Is it better to take one with everybody? One with everybody and one with just us?

(*She begins searching for it everywhere.*)

**RON.** What're you doing here?

**CHIP.** Lacey invited me.

(*The sound of a shoddy casserole dish dropping outside.*)

**SARA.** Shit. Ron, get the broom. GET THE BROOM!

(**SARA** *rushes offstage.* **RON** *follows her reluctantly.* **CHIP** *and* **ABBY** *stand together in the kitchen. Pause.)*

*(***ABBY** *adjusts the straps of her dress.* **CHIP** *coughs.)*

**ABBY.** Well, look at you! All dressed up!

**CHIP.** Yeah.

*(***CHIP** *looks uncomfortably around the kitchen.)*

*(Pause.* **ABBY** *takes a small step closer to him, he takes a step back.* **CHRISTOPHER** *enters, unseen by* **ABBY** *and* **CHIP***, with a spatula in his hand.)*

**ABBY.** You – um – you liking – you liking the training – you think you might stick around, or?

**CHIP.** Might go – someplace else.

*(pause)*

**ABBY.** Did you – did you, um – the other night – did you like –

**CHIP.** Yeah.

**ABBY.** You did?

**CHIP.** Yeah.

*(pause)*

**ABBY.** *(whispering)* It was crazy, it was so crazy.

I thought I was gonna die when you couldn't breathe cause you were gonna come so / hard

**CHIP.** I thought you said we weren't going to have to talk to about it.

**ABBY.** No, I know, I just – do you think I'm – I mean, do / you –

*(***CHRISTOPHER** *leaves, stunned. She steps towards* **CHIP***, touches his bicep. He jerks it away.)*

*(Awkwardly, she steps back.)*

You called me Jennifer.

**CHIP.** Did I?

**ABBY.** Yeah. You did.

*(***CHRISTOPHER***'s voice.)*

CHRISTOPHER. AB? ABB!! I LIT MYSELF ON FIRE –UH –
I THINK – A LITTLE BIT!

(ABBY *regards* CHIP, *then goes.* CHIP *finds food and
puts it in his mouth.*)

(RON *enters with an arm full of pink presents; a bow
on his head. Flowers. Embarrassed, he sets them on the
counter.*)

RON. She got so much shit. Look at all this shit she got.

POP POP. You boys, listen to me!

Worse part wasn't fear, fear's just part of it! The fear's
what puts the hairs on yer balls!  up thar –  it's how you
know who you are who er'ybody else is. Me, them. Me,
them. –

RON. Not now, Pop –

POP POP. I'M TELLIN YOU SOMETHIN!

Worse part was bein a way from *her*, seein that look on
her face when I go.

(*The microwave beeps, loud, annoying.*)

SARA (O.S.) RON, STIR THE DIP IN THE MIDDLE, WILL
YOU PLEASE?

(RON *rubs his eyes.*)

SARA. RON! YOU HEAR ME?

RON. I HEARD YOU!

(*He removes the dip gingerly from the microwave. It's
hot. It burns him. He drops it. It goes everywhere, all
over his apron. He kneels, grabs paper towels, tries to
scoop it back into the bowl. He stops, pissed, humiliated,
lost. He sits on the floor.* CHIP *watches him.*)

CHIP. You wanna get outta here? Let's get outta here.

(*He stops.*)

RON. And go where?

(SARA *enters.*)

CHIP. I know a place –

SARA. Go where?

> (RON *whips around and sees her.*)

SARA. You're not goin anywhere, Ron! We haven't even done cake yet! LACEY! GET BACK DOWN HERE!

RON. Baby, I just – I just am not / fit for –

> (RON *takes off the apron.*)

SARA. No, uh uh, don't you DARE!

CHIP. We / were just gonna –

SARA. I'm pregnant!

RON. No you're not.

> (*pause*)

SARA. I know.

> (LACEY *comes downstairs. She's changed back into her normal garb.*)

SARA. Lacey, where's your party dress? Goddamnit, goddamnit –

RON. Hey, happy birthday, Lacey.

> (*He reaches behind the fridge. He pulls out a rifle with a bow on it. She takes it, in awe.*)

LACEY. …Cool…..

SARA. What the hell is that?

RON. It's what she wants.

SARA. That doesn't mean you GIVE it to her! Lacey, get out there to your party. Come ere.

> (*She takes the gun.*)

You are NOT bringing a gun out to your party. Go out there and say hi. Go ahead and open what Granny and Grandpa sent you, it looks big! And find my camera and we're gonna take a family picture if it's the last thing I do. Daddy'll be right there, just go on out, hell, whatever.

> (LACEY *feels the heat between her parents, considers commenting, but then gives up and goes.*)

LACEY. *(on her way out)* Thanks, Daddy.

*(She sets down her gun and heads into the party.)*

*(SARA inspects the sad thing of dip on the floor.)*

SARA. My pretty dip. My pretty, pretty dip.

RON. Baby, I –

SARA. Don't you dare touch me cause I'm on fire right now.

*(She cries. She stops. She picks herself off the floor, drying her eyes. She scoops the dip back into the bowl, desperately. With a spoon, she smooths it, good as new.)*

WHO'S HUNGRY?

*(She carries the dip out to the party.)*

*(RON and CHIP are left alone in the kitchen with POP POP.)*

POP POP. You go, you break her heart, that's all.
Bah. What'm I sayin.

*(POP POP struggles to get out of his chair.)*

What am I doin here, what am I doin in this chair, get me outta here? GET ME OUTTA HERE!

*(RON and CHIP watch, horrified. He gives up, tears come to his eyes. He looks directly at RON.)*

*(Beat. RON heads towards the door, fast. CHIP follows. He returns, grabs a case of Miller from the fridge, then leaves. POP POP watches them go.)*

*(ABBY pulls CHRISTOPHER inside from the deck, leading him by the hand. CHRISTOPHER is silent.)*

ABBY. Come here, sit down.

*(She sits him in a chair, inspects the burn on his forearm. She gets a wet rag and applies it to the burn, tending to him.)*

There you go.

CHRISTOPHER. I can't believe I burned myself. Um. That's pretty bad ass, huh? I could've died.

ABBY. Pretty stupid.

CHRISTOPHER. Well that was the closest I've come, at least, okay, let me revel in it.

ABBY. Fine, okay.

*(She takes the rag off, inspects the wound. Their faces are close. His heart breaks.)*

CHRISTOPHER. Ab, did you –

ABBY. What?

*(CHRISTOPHER is silent.)*

CHRISTOPHER. Um – Do you love me?

*(ABBY hesitates.)*

ABBY. You know I do.

CHRISTOPHER. Cause I, um –
If you ever – I just want to have you, I don't want to like – just, do you?

ABBY. Yeah.

*(CHRISTOPHER nods, convincing himself. He sniffs. )*

CHRISTOPHER. Okay, cool. Just checking. That's all I need to know.

*(She kisses him tenderly. She takes him upstairs. POP POP sits alone.)*

POP POP. Bah.

*(beat)*

Barbara!

*(SARA rushes back into the kitchen, wielding her camera, pulling LACEY by the hand.)*

SARA. RON, I FOUND MY CAMERA, I LEFT IT IN THE BATH –

*(She looks around.)*

Ron? Where'd he go?

*(The sound offstage of tires pealing off. SARA looks out the window. She sits in a chair, dejected. LACEY approaches her grandfather.)*

**POP POP.** BARBARA.

**LACEY.** Where'd Daddy go?

**SARA.** I – um – ice. I think he went to get some ice. Go back into the party, I'm sure he'll be right back.

*(**LACEY** looks at her mother. She doesn't believe her. She's not yet old enough to argue for the truth, so she retreats. **SARA** lights a cigarette.)*

# VI.

*(Dark, that night.* **CHIP** *and* **RON** *with a case of a beer, have climbed to the top of a massive gas tank. They stand with their AK-47s, alert, drunk, but serious.)*

*(They face out.)*

**CHIP.** Ready?

**RON.** Ready.

**CHIP.** GO.

*(They field strip their guns. They both know it by heart.* **CHIP** *finishes first, and holds the weapon above his head. He is breathing hard.)*

**CHIP.** *(struggling to breathe)* VICTORY!

**RON.** You cheated!

**CHIP.** *(serious)* I fuckin never cheat.

**RON.** Alright, alright, you got skill.

**CHIP.** *Mad* skill.

*(***CHIP*** *reaches for his inhaler. He breathes in desperately, then embarrassed, puts it back in his pocket.* **RON** *watches in amazement until* **CHIP** *regains himself.)*

**RON.** Chip, fuckin A, you gotta –

**CHIP.** *(gulping for air)* What?

**RON.** Nothin, I just think you gotta – maybe you're not fit for –

**CHIP.** I AM.

**RON.** Alright.

*(***CHIP*** *breathes deep, regains himself. He finishes the last warm swig of his beer, reaches for another, hands one to* **RON***.)*

**CHIP.** You get that job?

**RON.** It was these two kids half my age interviewin me. They said, thank you for your service. They said, what other experience you got?

RON. *(cont.)* I said, whaddya mean, what OTHER experience?

They wrote stuff down, they nodded at me. They showed me around.

I kissed their fuckin asses. I told them what I team player I was and how interested I was in ceiling fans. I waited for them to call. I waited past 3 days for them to call. They said they were gonna call if I got it.

(**RON** *leans on the railing and looks over the edge.*)

CHIP. Fuck em.

RON. Yeah, fuck em.

Hell, what am I gonna do, sell health insurance? Shoot some deer on the weekends, jump outta airplanes for sport, push papers around, ride an elevator up one freakin floor? Hell nah!

CHIP. Hell *nah*. That's not where we belong.

RON. Yeah, We belong all through time, back to the first time somebody said, *I'm scared and I'm too weak to protect myself.* Back to the first someone said, *I'm pissed for good reason, I got justice on my side.*

CHIP. What are your skills if you can't use em?

RON. Like goin up to a violinist, choppin his hands off.

Nah, you gotta take what God has given you and use it, don't let it waste or atrophy.

CHIP. That's *right*.

RON. Semper Fi, right? That's what you say?

CHIP. SEMPER FI.

RON. Travel the world –

CHIP. Meet people of interesting cultures / and

RON. And kill them!

(*They laugh together, nostalgically.* **RON** *moves close to the edge of the tank.*)

CHIP. Don't stand so close, man.

RON. Damn, we're up real high, look.

CHIP. I don't wanna look.

**RON.** What, you scared?

**CHIP.** It's not natural to be up the air. I don't wanna fall off a some shit. I don't wanna die an arbitrary death, I'd want it to mean something.

**RON.** Yeah.

**CHIP.** Man, remember in basic when you're laying in the dust for hours shootin at a hole and you just wish somebody would come up to you and say, *Prove it, fucker!* and then you get to *prove* it.

*(yelling into the dark)*

PROVE IT, FUCKER!

*(He shoots his gun into the air. It goes off.)*

**RON.** DAMNIT! Are you crazy, man?

**CHIP.** What?

**RON.** I thought your safety was on?

**CHIP.** Hell nah, tricked you, I'm sly.

**RON.** Just be careful, man, you got skills –

**CHIP.** MAD skills –

**RON.** Yeah, just be careful with your mad skills.

**CHIP.** I am.

*(He takes the gun, aims at something. RON stares out into the night.)*

**RON.** Chip.

**CHIP.** What?

**RON.** I talked to the head recruiter.

**CHIP.** *(eagerly)* Yeah? And?

**RON.** I'm sorry.

**CHIP.** What?

**RON.** He said no. He said –

**CHIP.** What, what'd he say?

**RON.** ....That there he was nothing he could do. That your – weakness – would prevent you – from – *(beat)* I'm sorry.

*(A moment. **CHIP** breaths deep, steady.)*

**CHIP.** I don't care. That ain't gonna stop me.

See, We got a whole lotta people counting on us.

**RON.** You really think somebody would bomb this thing?

**CHIP.** There's some somebody somewhere who would do most anything.

*(beat)*

**RON.** What is this, half a mile a tanks a gas the size of a Olympic swimmin pools? Bomb this one tower, light up the rest, half the state gone in a second.

**CHIP.** All that tobacco, all those doughnuts.

**RON.** And people too.

*(beat)*

Maybe we deserve it.

**CHIP.** What?

**RON.** You ever think, maybe we deserve it? Whole country full a assholes, rich assholes, bad fathers – I can't even do a party – I can't even do my daughter's party –

**CHIP.** Hay, watch it.

**RON.** Killers and whores.

**CHIP.** Whose side are you on?

**RON.** I'm just sayin that if you stop and think about it, some a the things *we* done –

*(**CHIP** points his gun at **RON**. **RON** freezes.)*

**CHIP.** That's my country you're talking about.

**RON.** What the hell, are you crazy?

**CHIP.** That's my pride and all I *got!*

**RON.** Chip, come on –

**CHIP.** It's all I GOT!

**RON.** Oh what, you wanna shoot me?

**CHIP.** No – I jes – I jes wanna –

**RON.** What, you wanna what, you wanna shoot somebody?

**CHIP.** I JUST WANNA DO SOMETHIN!

**RON.** WHAT, LIKE SHOOT AT SOMEBODY?

**CHIP.** NO!

**RON.** PUT YOUR GUN DOWN!

*(But he doesn't. **RON** attempts to grab it from him. There is a struggle. **CHIP** is winning, but suddenly, he really can't breathe. He tries to ignore this, but finally releases the gun, closes his eyes, breathing deep to regain control. This takes a few moments. **CHIP** sits. Softly, **RON** leans the gun against the tank.)*

**RON.** You alright there, soldier?

**CHIP.** It's just all I got.

**RON.** I get that.

**CHIP.** I don't really have anything else.

*(beat)*

**RON.** What the hell are we doin? Look at us. Chip, what in the HELL are we doin?

*(**CHIP** stares out into the night. The soft sounds of traffic from the freeway.)*

**RON.** We should prolly head back, it's getting late.

*(beat)*

I don't wanna head back.

**CHIP.** Me neither.

**RON.** I'm gonna do another tour. I don't know how, but I'm gonna get on one.

*(beat)*

It's not that I don't love them. I love them so much.

**CHIP.** I know.

**RON.** It's just I got other things to give.

**CHIP.** Me too.

**RON.** Somebody better give me something to do real soon, Chip.

**CHIP.** We gotta do what we gotta do.

(**CHIP** *gets another beer. He hands one to* **RON**. *They sit, leaning against the tower.*)

**RON.** OohRah, Chip.

**CHIP.** OohRah, Sir.

(*They cheers.*)

## Epilogue

*(The kitchen, later that night. Remnants of the party. The oven light is on. They wait. )*

*(SARA sits at the table with her fifth glass of wine. She's just waiting. LACEY sits underneath the table wearing her Dad's T-shirt and tags, holding her gun which still has a bow on it. ABBY stands in a wedding dress.)*

ABBY. Does it make me look fat?

*(SARA shakes her head no and lights a cigarette.)*

SARA. I think we need a food processor.

ABBY. It like – pulls me *in* but in a way that makes me feel fat but maybe makes me look LESS fat.

SARA. You look good.

*(She smokes.)*

Where'd Chris go?

ABBY. Home. *(beat)*

Ron'll come back, don't worry.

SARA. Yeah.

ABBY. So you like it? It's not too bride-y?

SARA. You *are* a goddamn bride.

ABBY. I liked your wedding dress, yours was alright.

*(beat)*

*(SARA weeps. ABBY puts her hand on her head. SARA stops.)*

SARA. I cried my cigarette out.

*(Not knowing what to say, ABBY hands her a fresh one from the pack, and lights it for her. SARA looks at her phone.)*

SARA. He hasn't even called or anything.

*(Beat. She throws her phone.)*

Lacey, are you hungry?

Lacey.

SARA. *(cont.)* You have fun at your party? I thought it turned
out real nice. You get everything you want?

*(LACEY puts her head inside of the T-shirt.)*

Daddy'll be home real soon and tuck you into bed.

*(LACEY doesn't respond.)*

LACEY.

*(LACEY runs upstairs with the gun.)*

SARA. THAT BETTER NOT BE LOADED!

*(Silence. ABBY sits down at the table. This takes a
minute. ABBY hestitates, then lights a cigarette for herself.)*

What am I meant to do, sit around and wait?

ABBY. I'm just glad Chris isn't in the military.

SARA. I'm tired a waiting, I'm sick of it.

*(SARA and ABBY sit together. They smoke.)*

*(lights)*

Also by
**Bekah Brunstetter...**

**F\*cking Art**

**I Used to Write on Walls**

**Sick**

Please visit our website **samuelfrench.com** for complete
descriptions and licensing information.